A Flower in the Heart of the Painting

Stories by

Amy Krohn

Wiseblood Books

Milwaukee, Wisconsin

Cover Design: Dominic Heisdorf

Cover Image: Carl Larsson, *Flowers on the Windowsill.* 1894.

Interior Image: Paul Cézanne's *Sainte-Victoire Mountain.* Circa 1897.

Printed in the United States of America
Set in Arabic Typesetting

Library of Congress Cataloging-in-Publication Data
Krohn, Amy, 1981-
A Flower in the Heart of the Painting: stories/ Amy Krohn;
1. Krohn, Amy, 1981-
2. Fiction

ISBN-13: 978-0615829500
ISBN-10: 0615829503

Dedicated to Mom and Dad

TABLE OF CONTENTS

That day ended the romance of our marriage; the old feeling from thereon became but a precious and irrecoverable remembrance; but a new feeling of love for my children and the father of my children laid the foundation of a new life and a quite different happiness; and that life and happiness have lasted to the present time.

—Leo Tolstoi, *Family Happiness*

On Eagle's Wings

Elizabeth Vande Wal drove her car through the Horicon Marsh auto route and parked in her usual spot beside the picnic table. She got out, holding her head up to feel the breeze and to sniff the marshy air. It smelled like the bag of potting soil she kept in her garage. Leaves on the trees were just unfurling, making the wooded area seem dressed up for a special occasion. A jagged V of geese honked overhead and the rattling call of a sandhill crane sounded from somewhere deep in the marsh. The sun, though not hot, shone brightly, and Elizabeth reached back into the car for her sunglasses. She closed the door quietly because she did not like to disturb the wildlife. So many young couples took their noisy children on this short walk through the marsh, and their clattering feet and loud, happy shouts did not seem well-suited to the serene stretch of marshland which served as a rare haven for so many different species of birds and other animals. Elizabeth went this way often, and she always stepped lightly along the boardwalk, only nodding politely to anyone who might greet her along the way.

This afternoon, though it was late and getting to be the time when nature-minded parents took their school children for a quick stint in the wilderness, Elizabeth was glad to see few vehicles in the parking lot. Today, though she stepped softly along the bright path, her thoughts hung heavy, and they filled her mind with clouds of unrest. Bitterness, a vice which plagued her till she felt devoured by it, began to uncoil and rattle its sinister tail. She knew all the warning signs, and after years of falling prey to this form of depression, she went fast to remedies that sometimes relieved the symptoms.

She had been sewing peacefully at the couch, barely a thought in her head beside those minimally necessary to count the correct number of stitches and find the right shade of thread amongst her large collection of spools and bundles. Then she realized she was hungry, but simultaneously felt despair at the thought of cooking another meal. What was the point of eating? She would only eat too much or too little and be uncomfortable again in a short time. After going on in this way for a few minutes, she firmly put down her sewing and fixed herself a snack of cheese and crackers. Then she resolutely donned her walking shoes, retrieved the car key from the nail beside her door, quickly and forcefully closed the door behind herself, as though to stop a pursuing enemy, and left for the Horicon Marsh. Some days, if she was fortunate enough to rise above her depression, she might walk around the block, or do some housecleaning, or simply open a window and stand in front of it, breathing the fresh air. These remedies usually helped, and sometimes they even chased the evil moods away. But Elizabeth knew her problems would always resurface, and it was this realization that dragged her spirits down, automatically, just as the breeze from the marsh lifted tendrils of her gray hair from her forehead and neck. Depression didn't leave; it hibernated. Bitterness couldn't be extracted, only placated. With all this evil residing in her heart, Elizabeth wilted under the false guilt of not being able to save herself, and then tears began to rise up in a fountain of self-pity. She closed her eyes for a moment, and steadied herself against the rope railing.

As she continued, calmer, across the floating boardwalk, she noticed the ducks dipping their heads into the water but did not appreciate them, not even really seeing them as *ducks* so much as mechanical movements in the water. Nor did she much care about the loons coasting past her. She strode along the edge of the marsh and entered the wooded portion of the trail. With a sigh, she sat down on the bench, staring glumly at a chipmunk who stood on hind legs beside a fallen branch.

As she sat, she heard the noises of people coming up from the opposite direction. Two voices: one male and animated, the other girlish and loud. She took notice of these voices because they seemed vaguely familiar. As the leaves on the trees were still young and frilly, Elizabeth could easily peer through the woods and see the couple walking along the twisting path. Her heart fluttered when she realized the two were her grandchildren, Lucas and Angela. Tom's kids. She watched them walk quickly toward her, but they were so involved in their conversation that they did not spy her on the bench. Suddenly Angela stopped and pointed at something in the woods. She sprang off the path and began to climb a leaning tree trunk so as to get a better view.

"Now hold on there!" Lucas protested, but soon he also was climbing the tree. They sat next to each other, Lucas, nearly a man, shading his eyes to follow where his twelve-year-old sister pointed at a yellow bird perched high in the treetops.

The bird flew out of view, but Elizabeth's grandchildren remained on the slanted tree trunk, swinging their legs and continuing a discussion of Angela's art project, which Elizabeth gathered to be a watercolor painting of a sunset. She was explaining it in minute detail to Lucas, who listened attentively and then said, "You keep painting like that, and then, when you get to high school and a teacher tells you that you have no talent, maybe you won't believe him."

"Did your teacher tell you that?" Angela asked.

"Yup." Lucas' back was turned to Elizabeth, but she sensed from his posture that he was squinting into the distance. "My choir teacher."

"But you love to sing!" Angela's voice rose in fury, startling some sparrows from the brush nearby. "He's a miserable liar. You have tons of talent."

"Thanks, Angie, but I supposed—and still suppose— that he was right. I told him I wanted to go to music school, take voice lessons and all that, and he shook his head and told me to think of a better idea. He said I'd never make it in music school. I don't have the right quality of voice."

Angela fumed loudly against the teacher until Lucas broke in. "But hey, don't be telling Dad about this because I never told him. You know he thinks I'm going to run the business with him. And maybe I will, too."

Elizabeth shrank back into her bench. She felt guilty for eavesdropping, and she did not want her grandchildren to find her there. They made a move to descend their tree trunk, and she decided to quietly retrace her steps. When they did encounter her, it was on the boardwalk, with the open breeze blowing across their surprised faces and making it difficult to talk for very long.

"Grandma!" Lucas exclaimed. "What are you doing here?"

Elizabeth did not pretend to be delighted to see them, because she believed in sincerity, but she did attempt a smile for their sakes. "Out walking, same as you, I presume."

Angela, who had always been shy around Elizabeth, asked tentatively, "Which way are you going?"

Elizabeth pointed to the wooded area where she had been sitting. "Nice day, isn't it?" She paused. "And how are you two doing?"

Lucas grinned. "Peachy!"

Angela only shrugged, and then said excitedly, "Oh look! A blue heron!"

They all turned to look. Gliding gracefully above the dead marsh grass from last season, the elusive great blue heron flapped its wings and rose into the air, taking itself further into the marsh and out of eyesight. The three of them stood watching the empty space where it had been. Elizabeth said, "I hope you say hello to your father for me. I rarely hear from him these days."

"We'll do that," Lucas said.

Angela stood stiffly, looking cold. She obviously wanted to keep going but wouldn't until the "grown-ups" had finished talking.

"You'd better keep going, now," Elizabeth said. "Have a good evening."

"You too, Grandma!" Lucas prodded Angela with a hand on her back, and the two waved and walked into the wind. Elizabeth watched them go, and then she disappeared into the woods for a second time.

She returned home in a thoughtful mood, less melancholic than earlier. She was thinking not about herself, but rather about Lucas and his idea that he wanted to be a singer. She had heard him sing; he often seemed to break out in song spontaneously. His voice was not cultured and maybe not even in tune, but it held the appeal of someone completely unashamed of being heard. This trait did not come from Elizabeth, and certainly not from Tom, who had always been a brooder. Lucas' mother, Marcia, had been the extrovert in the family. Boldly she came into their life, boldly she divorced them all. None of them had heard anything of her in at least five years. They assumed she was living in California, riding the backseat of a Harley with that other man.

Divorces and bad marriages held a special seat of contempt in Elizabeth's heart. The Vande Wals seemed doomed to marry badly and suffer as a result and, not at all unexpectedly, the demise of Tom's marriage left him a hard, angry man. Elizabeth still loved him as she would always love her children, but she preferred not to see him often, and she assumed the reverse was true as well.

Her other son, Jake, had married twice, divorced twice, and now lived in Illinois with a beautician and her three children. Elizabeth didn't recall their names. She sent them a little money for Christmas gifts every year, but that was as far as it went. Jake called a few times a year and noticeably said nothing about the people he lived with.

Elizabeth herself had never divorced. No, she had stuck with Gilbert to the bitter end.

Disgusted with her train of thought, Elizabeth moved in a half-run into the kitchen to attack the dirty dishes that filled the sink. She flushed out the water until it was hot, poured in a stream of dish soap, began to immerse silverware into the froth. The dirty dishes ran out before she had cleared her head of its own filthy blackness. She flung open the refrigerator and pulled out the carton of eggs and a block of cheese. She scraped vigorously at the cheese with the shredder, and, when that was done, she made herself an omelet, concentrating so hard on the task that deep furrows appeared between her eyebrows and at the sides of her mouth, which was set in a frown.

Satisfied in some small way, Elizabeth sat down at the table and forced herself to pray, eat, and clear up the dishes. She glanced at the clock and almost cried in frustration when she saw it was only five-thirty. Sleep would not come to her rescue for hours yet. She could feel herself disappearing into the cloud of depression, coming closer and closer to its center. Her shoulders ached with the heaviness she felt.

In desperation, she took up her sewing again. She threw it down. This very couch, with the delicate, twisted vine

7

design she had admired so much at the store, this very couch was where Gilbert spent his last miserable days until hospice brought the hospital bed, and the oxygen tank, and the bed pan. By then he was unrecognizable, just a dried-up wreck of flesh, sucking in his breaths like a machine on its last legs. By then he couldn't scream at her, or accuse her of wanting to kill him, or cry pitifully for his mama over and over again.

Elizabeth left the couch, walked blindly away from it, searched for something to put her hands on, and then pulled open the drawers of the bureau where she kept her sewing things. She rummaged about, not knowing what she was looking for. At the back of one drawer, she came across something forgotten. It was a cross-stitch she had begun once and then abandoned. A picture of an eagle soaring above some pine trees and the verse, "They who wait for the Lord shall renew their strength; they shall mount up with wings like eagles; they shall run and not be weary; they shall walk and not faint." She ran her fingers over the patches of completed stitches. She remembered, now, that she had begun it when Tom was a year old and she was pregnant with Jake. She had been so tired, and, even then, so afflicted by her moodiness that she couldn't sleep well. A friend gave her the cross-stitch kit, and Elizabeth worked on it during Tom's naps, forcing herself to sit and relax so she wouldn't bring harm to the new baby. The needle was still threaded with white thread and weaved into the edge of the canvas for safekeeping.

She sat down in a nearby chair, unfolded the brittle paper on which the pattern was printed, and pulled out the needle. Carefully, she counted some stitches, and began drawing the white thread back and forth through the canvas.

Gilbert had always wanted children. "Fill the house up with the pitter-patter of little feet," he would say, giving her a hug. At the beginning, he had been tickled to find himself married. When Tom was born, he had laughed in delight like a prospector discovering gold in his pan. He couldn't believe his good fortune. When the fortune began turning (after Jake came three miscarriages, and then they had given up), Gilbert turned to his work, spent endless hours at his construction job sites, talked about nothing else when he was at home. As the years went by, he turned further and further away from Elizabeth, even to the point of attending a different church by himself, going to restaurants for meals while Elizabeth ate at the table with the boys. When they finally bought a television, he watched it so he didn't have to talk to Elizabeth.

She had been hurting so much. The anger, the depression, the sorrow of losing her love. She went through times when she cried long and hard every time the boys were safely asleep. She didn't care if Gilbert heard her. If she woke him up, he only turned his back and started snoring again.

Of course, she didn't try to go it alone. At one point she sought help from her minister. He had counseled her from the Bible, showing her that depression was a lack of trust in God. He had asked if she thought God was in control of everything in her life. She had said, "Yes." He had said, "Then live like it." She couldn't. Or, she could, but it didn't fix things the way the pastor insisted it would. Something in her was broken, and trust didn't mean healing. When she came back to the minister with these words, he had told her that it was because of sin. Jesus came to conquer all the brokenness of the world. He had left her wondering if she was truly a Christian.

For the boys' sakes, she had carried on as if she was. She took them to church, helped them learn their Sunday School verses, prayed with them at the table, and read them Bible stories at bedtime. During that entire period of their childhoods she had lived in two distinct identities. On one side of the imaginary dividing line, she had lived as she had been raised, and this was the person she made certain the boys knew her as. On the other side, in the other identity, she lived in fear and doubt, within that horrible cloud where the snake of bitterness thrived and choked off any real contentment. Elizabeth hated pretense, so these two different lives spoiled her chances of happiness. She was always pretending.

At nine o'clock, Elizabeth got up, stretched her legs, locked her doors, took a shower, and then debated about going to bed. She decided not to, and instead she returned to the chair with the cross-stitch. As she began threading the needle again, she determined to finish it. She would not sleep until the last stitch had been made.

The eagle on the cross-stitch reminded her of the blue heron she had seen earlier that day. On a good day, she would have marveled at the sight of the heron, sending up a little prayer of thanks for God's beautiful handiwork. But as this had not been a good day, the heron only made her think of Lucas and the secret he held from Tom. It was well that he kept his dreams to be a singer beyond his father's ears. Tom would certainly not approve of it. Tom believed in working with his hands, just like his own father had taught him, and just like his son *should*. Elizabeth thought with irony at how many pains she had taken to keep her boys safe from the bad influences of their father. It had all proved useless. Tom acted just like Gilbert in so many, in too many ways. How would Lucas turn out? He was too essentially different from his father and grandfather to think like them. But he could be broken. He could be bitter. His jauntiness and the kindness he showed to his sister could be crippled and reduced to a shadow of what they were.

Gilbert had slowly succumbed to a lamed spirit, just as his body had succumbed to the cancer growing inside him. But the cancer had taken over quickly, leaving only the tombstone in the cemetery with Elizabeth's name on one side; below that came her birth date, a dash, and an empty space waiting to be filled. Elizabeth visited out of duty, but when she went she tried to concentrate on the weather, or the planter of flowers beside the stone. If she let her mind go its own way, she felt as if Gilbert was calling to her from the grave in that hurt, accusing voice, "Lizzie, you did this to me. You have always hated me. You will be glad when I die. You never wanted to please me; only yourself. You have always hated me."

Did she hate him? Sometimes, yes, she believed she did. How could she not?

There had, she paused, snipping a thread with her teeth, been moments of partial redemption in her life. Jake had shown great promise. He had been the valedictorian of his high school class. He had chosen to study law, and this was a grand and delightful idea for his mother to contemplate during her lonely, grim days at home. He had married pretty Ella Mae from Mississippi, and Elizabeth showed so much friendship to her new daughter-in-law that she was tempted to see herself as cause of the early divorce. And then Jake switched to studying business. And then, a little later, he quit college altogether and worked as a construction worker. Just like his brother Tom. Just like his father.

Elizabeth had had a few friends of her own, ladies from church. The one who had given her the cross-stitch had been so generous in all things. She had shared recipes, gossip, books, stories of her own successful children. She had shared so much that Elizabeth had started giving things back, not returning her phone calls, purposely ignoring her at church. That woman, that generous, nameless woman, still lived nearby, but she may as well have moved to another state, or into the graveyard which was her and Elizabeth's shared destiny. All cords of friendship had been snapped.

At this thought, Elizabeth's resolve to finish the cross-stitch almost crumbled. She felt her face get hot, and the tears built up behind her eyes. She tugged fiercely at her stitching, and a knot formed in the thread which she couldn't see clearly enough to remove. The tears fell onto the cross-stitch, and she thought again of Lucas, and bravely took a few deep breaths, wiping her face with the back of her hand. What an old crybaby she was! She couldn't even do this bit of work without crying. And this would go to Lucas, her grandson, the one who would be a singer, if she had anything to do about it.

She wouldn't have anything to do about it. She finally picked out the knot and resumed her stitching. Her relations with her two grandchildren were strained. Angela, sweet girl, acted as though she was afraid of her. Lucas felt some sort of duty toward her, but he didn't really love her the way so many grandchildren love their grandma. So many times she had heard, "You are so lucky for having your grandchildren nearby. Mine are halfway across the world." Each time she heard this Elizabeth felt as if it might be better if her grandchildren were far away, but she kept her lips closed. From the safety of distant lands they might write to each other, and in their letters they could say things they could never say in person. Elizabeth might have some sort of influence over her grandchildren. She might be able to worm a small hole into their heart. There she could settle in as the beloved grandma instead of the strange grandma who lived across town in the sad house where Grandpa died. She often felt as if her grandchildren and children pitied her, and then didn't know how to express it.

So there she was, alone, madly stitching a cross-stitch into the wee hours of the night, her eyes weary from being held open, her fingers sore from the needlework. She finished it, finally, and then she decided she might as well go the whole way and frame it, too. She found a suitable frame in her bureau drawers. She trimmed the frayed edges of the canvas, taped the corners in the back, fitted it into the frame. Removing a picture from her wall, she hung the cross-stitch on the empty nail.

Stepping back to admire her work, she tripped over a rug and fell hard on her hip. She passed out from the pain, and awoke to even more agony as the sun, streaming through her Venetian blinds, revealed that it was mid-morning. Elizabeth slowly dragged herself to the desk with the phone. When she had it in her hands, she was so exhausted and in such pain that she couldn't think clearly. She dialed Tom's number. When Lucas answered, a little droopy because he enjoyed sleeping in on Saturday mornings, Elizabeth cried into the phone, apologizing for all the things she had done to ruin his life. "I've ruined your life," she sobbed. "You'll never be a singer now. It was me. I didn't do enough to raise the boys right. It was me!"

Thankfully, Lucas couldn't understand much of what she said. He thought it sounded like his grandma, and he hurried to tell his dad. They rushed over and knocked on the locked doors until finally Tom had to break in. They found Elizabeth still cradling the telephone, crying, rocking awkwardly back and forth on the floor. Frowning deeply so as to hold back his own tears, Tom put his arms around his mother. "You'll be okay," he said. "We'll get help for you."

Lucas stood back, watching, hardly believing that this was happening. Those unreal memories of his grandpa shriveled up on his deathbed, the image of his grandma crying and crippled on the floor, the sight of his cold, silent father hugging her and trying not to cry and failing. He couldn't think how everything had all turned out this way.

An Abstract Copy of My Heart

Genevieve offered Allie a wonderful hard chair, new, firm cushions, not low to the ground like so many chairs in Allie's own house. After driving along the winding back roads of northern Wisconsin for nearly two hours, Allie's knees felt as sore as they did after a morning in her studio, after her first aspirins faded. The chair, its beige and mauve material not even dusty, faded, or threadbare yet, had rounded armrests upon which Allie placed both her arms. Moses, made of wood, cement, and a little paint, stood three feet tall at one side of the chair, and two or three dozen Israelites gathered around the other side. The crude statues overrunning the whole room had taken her by surprise when Genevieve first ushered her inside, but now that she was sitting comfortably in the new chair, her legs stretched out and crossed at the ankles, her knees only aching in a minor, manageable way, Allie ran her eye over the biblical characters, admiring the deep shadows in the crowd of Israelites and the simple lines of the smaller, shelved statuettes running across one wall. Her artist's eye caught every detail. There was no fussiness in the long, cement faces, the painted eyes, beards, and unsmiling mouths, or the natural drape of hoods and robes, all dependent on the shape of the wood. In fact, they looked as if they had stepped in from the woods and gathered here a short time before Allie. Like her, they were quietly waiting for direction.

The sound of a telephone clicking back into its receiver came from the room connected to this crowded sitting room. Genevieve stopped in the doorway, touching the wall with one of her thin, bony hands. She was a slight woman with shoulder-length white hair pulled back in a big, rusting barrette. She stooped a little, but not much. In their white sneakers her feet were very straight and neat for an old woman. Allie judged Genevieve to be in her late seventies, maybe eighty, the age her own mother would have been this year. Allie was fifty-seven, but she often felt as if her bones had aged too fast, pulling the rest of her body out of whack: her aching joints, a touch of skin cancer a few years ago, the bulk that collected around her waist and thighs ever since she bore her son, Wendell.

"I called my son-in-law about the tree," Genevieve said, her voice brittle on some words and liquid on others, as if her mouth salivated unevenly. "He'll make sure it's taken care of."

The tree was the reason Allie was sitting in Genevieve's house among her people. She had been driving home from a wedding until a fallen tree halted her progress. Genevieve's driveway, winding out of the woods, nearly obscured by the brown and orange autumn leaves layering the ground, had been the closest. Allie had almost turned back to find another driveway when she pulled up next to the old, peeling house, its porch posts tilted, giving the dark gray roof a sagging, crooked appearance. A weathered wooden sign affixed to the door had said in faded letters, "Green Inn, Please Ring the Bell." An old cowbell hung from the doorknob on a frayed twine string, but the windows were clean, and Allie had seen Genevieve's small, pale face peering out of one of them, the white popping from the dark, reminding her of the Gainsborough portrait print she had hanging in her guest room. In the portrait, the woman held the viewer's gaze with a bland but imperious stare befitting her stylish attire. In the window, Genevieve had watched Allie from similar hooded eyes above a long nose and pressed lips. Then she had turned to open the door, her face retreating into the shadows of the house.

Genevieve walked slowly to the other chair in the room, a wicker-seated wooden rocker. Although it was nicked and dented in several places, she sat down with that trust Allie had learned to have in her own chairs: concentrate on the floor in front of your feet and lower yourself into the chair, sure that it will still be there. When Genevieve sat in the rocker, Allie could tell it was her chair of choice. She rocked as if she had been doing it for thirty years at the same speed. Allie counted. One complete rock in three seconds, the old woman's white sneakers moving but not lifting off the ground. As the chair rocked backward, her blue pants rode up, revealing dark nylons. Allie smiled, remembered going through her own mother's drawers, which had included at least twenty pairs of knee-high nylons rolled up into meshy balls. She had thrown most of them away, but kept a few for washing mirrors and windows.

Genevieve was looking out the window behind Allie, over the heads of the Israelites. The light coming in illuminated the skin right above her eyebrows and the side of her nose. Her eyes, mouth, and chin sunk into her face. Her vacant expression and rhythmic rocking made Allie guess she had momentarily forgotten her company; however, Genevieve cleared her throat with a little humming sound and said, "I'm glad you're here. This time of morning I get lonely for people. When David and I ran the inn, the guests would sit around the table, drinking coffee and chatting while I washed the breakfast dishes and listened." She smiled, revealing a set of false teeth that curved in too quickly as though they were too small for her mouth. "I felt guilty eavesdropping, but told myself God wouldn't want me to bang the dishes around too hard, giving everyone headaches."

"Ah," Allie said, "Green Inn. I saw the sign on your door. Did you get many guests out here?" She thought of the winding rural road and the almost non-existent traffic. In fact, the tree across the road looked natural there, hardly an obstruction, like it would across a small hiking path.

"Hunters, mostly. We were busiest in the fall. Sometimes the motel in Park Falls filled up and sent folks out here." She shrugged her shoulders, never missing a beat in her rocking. "But that was fifteen, twenty years ago."

Allie thought back twenty years. What had she been doing then? Wendell, age three, had been bent on rummaging through all her cupboards and drawers, in spite of all her corrective efforts. It was the year he had tasted some of her acrylic paints and had to be hospitalized. The memories came into the clear. Allie had painted big, blown-up abstractions of leaves and berries on huge canvases. They had sold well, and it had been the first time since Wendell was born that she really produced anything. She wondered now if she had sacrificed too much time with Wendell. He had been a quiet child. Mischievous, but not demanding constant attention. He had been cute too, with rosy cheeks and floppy white-blond hair like his father's. Jerry hadn't spent much time with his son, either. Teaching and writing his doctoral thesis had kept him ten hours a day at the university. Had it been his thesis, then, or his book about naturalism in Germany? Whatever the case, he had spent a fair amount of his summers in Munich.

Genevieve sneezed, and for an instant her pale face wrinkled and distorted into the face of an ogre. She pulled a neatly folded yellow hankie from the cuff of her blouse and wiped her nose.

"Bless you," Allie said. "You don't have a cold, do you?"

Genevieve folded up the hankie and hid it in her clenched hand. "No, I don't believe so. A sneeze is good for the system, they say."

Allie nodded. "Gets the devil out."

Genevieve stopped rocking and closed her eyes. When she opened them again, she appeared to be speaking to the Israelites. "The devil is not welcome here."

Allie glanced at the figures to see what their response would be. They did not move. Allie pointed at them. "You know, these are really quite amazing. Did you make these?"

She nodded. "They keep my hands busy. And my heart welcomes the company."

The phone rang then, and Genevieve placed her feet square in front of her, one hand firmly on each arm of the chair.

"Would you like me to get that?" Allie asked.

"No, I'll get it." The old woman lifted herself from the chair with a soft grunt. By the time she reached the telephone, it had rung five times, and Allie watched her slow procession with admiration. She hoped she would have that much mobility and presence of mind when she was that age.

She stretched out her aching legs and stared at them. Perhaps Genevieve wasn't as sane as she seemed. *My heart welcomes the company...* Did she talk to the statues, like they were guests at her inn? The smaller statuettes on the shelves depicted various Bible scenes, such as the Sermon on the Mount, Adam and Eve, with a serpent curled around Eve's neck, Abraham tying Isaac to an altar. Allie searched the room for tools, but didn't find any. Her workshop must be in a different room, and certainly the old woman must have help, especially with the cement work. Even Allie needed help these days with the construction components of her art. While building frames and stretching canvases had never been easy for her, these seemed impossible now. Sometimes Jerry came into her studio before supper and helped her clean brushes and wash the table. Her hands were not arthritic yet, but they felt thicker and clumsier than they had in the old days when she could spend four or five consecutive hours painting, rinsing out the brushes as needed, unscrewing sticky paint tubes with ease.

Something clattered in the next room, and Allie realized Genevieve had hung up and was making something in the kitchen. Getting out of the chair, she decided to be more respectful of her hostess. The lady might be overly religious, but she had a sensitive touch. Allie rubbed her hand over an Israelite's face. It was modeled smooth, the nose rounded and large, the eyes concave.

The kitchen was also crowded with figures, so that the only openings were a path to the sink, the stove, and the refrigerator. Even the counters were filled, some of the figurines acting as bookends for recipe books and props for drying dishrags. Genevieve stood at the stove, putting on a pot of water. She smiled at Allie.

"I thought we'd have some tea. Do you like tea?"

Allie nodded. "Sure I do. I used to drink coffee, but then I switched when I was pregnant with my son."

"You have children?" Genevieve asked, wiping a canister lid with a damp cloth.

"One. His name is Wendell. He's twenty-three now, living out in New York."

"New York." In her mouth, the name had a foreign ring, as though it existed on the other side of an ocean. She sighed and glanced at the telephone. "That was my son-in-law on the phone. He says the county workers are going to work on that tree as soon as possible. He offered to do the work himself, but the county wouldn't let him. They did say they would give him the wood, if he wanted it."

Allie patted a female figure on the head. "Does that mean more work for you? I really am astounded by the number of these statues. Do you ever sell any?"

Genevieve shifted the teapot on the stove. "No, no. They're more like a love offering." She paused to take two teacups from a cupboard. "I give them to people

21

sometimes, but mostly they're my testimony, the small thing I can do for the Lord."

That sort of devotion. Allie thought back to her college-age zeal. Except it wasn't God she had worshiped; it was her boyfriend Mel, who had seemed like a god, self-sacrificing and great. Rather than developing his own work to the high standards he was capable of, Mel poured his energies into showing Allie how to control the paint and let the paint control her, how to bring life from a stick of charcoal and bring a stick of charcoal to life. Allie had loved Mel, and she had worked hard under his instruction, staying in the studios days on end, always producing, always trying to impress *him*, caring little about what her professors said. In a way, he *had* been her god. When he quit school because of failing grades, she felt he had somehow failed her, and it disgusted her. He told her *she* had the real talent, and he wanted to live with her, help her achieve excellence. But her faith in him had been broken. She left him her final year. And then, the year after she graduated, she floundered, throwing away almost all of her work in disgust, and getting a job as a secretary. One night she had painted a simple watercolor of her cat, and nearly tore it in two, imagining Mel's response: "It's got good lines, but where's the importance? You could have done this two years ago, girly-girl. Keep raising the bar." But then she had looked at it again and decided she really liked it. It wasn't kitsch. She wouldn't have done it two years ago. Something about the roll of the sleeping cat and the wash of orange next to green looked Oriental, and Allie had never studied Oriental art. She kept the cat, took out several books from the library, and worked nights at a series of watercolors and ink drawings, which later became her first show.

In the kitchen filled with Genevieve's love offerings, Allie found it hard to believe that Genevieve was ever separated from God. She didn't look like she ever floundered, but then, she was very old and perhaps several housefuls of apostles and judges and kings had been chopped for firewood already. Allie wondered where Genevieve had learned the craft, and if she had done it all her life. She was about to ask something along this line when the old woman handed her a teacup and saucer and motioned her to follow the path into the dining room, which wasn't quite as crowded as the other rooms.

"Your son," Genevieve said when they sat at an old, dark table, scratched and worn from years of use, "does he go to college?"

Allie bobbed the tea bag in her cup, staring at the stained water. "Wendell tried college once. He didn't like it. He's in New York now, just because he thought he'd like New York. He doesn't call often." She sighed and took a small sip. "I thought maybe he'd make a go of his art. He has talent."

Wendell had grown up among easels, canvases, boxes of vine charcoal, coffee tins filled with paintbrushes. He had gone through a gummy-eraser phase during which he fiddled with gummy erasers constantly, pulling them apart, smashing them together, kneading them like bread dough. Instruments of art were his toys. At age six, Wendell had pinned up his crayon drawings and Allie had critiqued them as she would for her occasional student. In middle school and high school he won several art contests, one of them national. He had everything going for him, even a free ride to the Chicago Art Institute.

Allie shook her head, thinking of his last phone call. He'd said he found a couple roommates to help pay rent, and he was working weekends as a night auditor at a hotel. She glanced out Genevieve's window at the leafy woodland. The view from Wendell's hotel probably didn't have a single tree in it. And it wouldn't have such holy company either, she thought, smiling at a female holding a baby near the window.

"That's Mary," Genevieve said, setting down her teacup. "She's the only Mary I ever made."

Allie stood to examine the Mary sculpture up close. It was made of the same wood as most of the others, except the baby (a lump in Mary's arms) still had some bark on it, and he was coarse and unfinished. This drew Allie back to the fact that the sculptures were once trees, things which were not man-made. Some sculptors left the human signature of fingerprints and tool marks, but Genevieve left God's signature.

"It's your best," Allie said.

Genevieve laughed, the sound coming from her throat like a dry cough. "How do you know? You haven't seen them all."

"I'm an artist," Allie said, realizing her hostess didn't know. "I'm doing color studies right now. The painting I'm working on is two feet by three feet and consists of five-inch blue stripes." She moved her hands to demonstrate the dimensions. "I keep thinking of the ocean and different levels of water." And thinking, and thinking

24

until she was tired of thinking. She wanted to try something new, but nothing new ever came to her tired mind. She looked at the world around, but everything seemed so distant that it could be translated into little else than patterns of stripes. Life had become something she looked in on or heard about, or sometimes analyzed, but she didn't have much to do with it anymore. Wendell had to take care of himself now. Her relationship with Jerry slid along the same easy lines they had shared for years. Her art career was well-established. Even the sensitive job of caring for her mother had ended.

The old woman swallowed her tea and licked her lips. "Stripes," she said, in much the same way she had said "New York" earlier.

Allie smiled because Genevieve's reaction to abstract art was like her own mother's. When Allie had started selling work and becoming well-known, first in the Midwest and then across the nation, Allie's mother had been astonished. When Allie had showed her an article in *Contemporary Art* that had the words "Newcomer Allie Oxford" splashed across a reproduction of one of her landscape abstractions, her mother had pushed up her eyeglasses and looked at the painting, asking, "Why is that good? It looks like something you did in first grade." She wasn't rude, Allie had to tell herself, even now, just confused.

Returning to her seat at the table, Allie thought of the art her mother had liked: pastoral scenes of cabins by a river, deer under autumn trees, a horse and buggy on a country road. Those old oils were wrapped up in Allie's attic right now, stuck between boxes of her mother's recipe books and sewing patterns. Looking around Genevieve's dining room, Allie nearly laughed. What would her children do with all these sculptures when Genevieve passed away? It'd be a shame to burn such an extensive collection, but no amount of attic space would hold all this.

As if she knew what Allie was thinking, Genevieve coughed long and hard, her frail body racked by the effort, both hands at her mouth. When the coughing stopped, Genevieve sat still, slumped against the back of her chair, concentrating on breathing. Allie watched her awhile, and then felt as if she was invading the older woman's privacy. She turned her eyes back to the Mary statue. What was it about the sculpture that set it apart from the rest? It wasn't merely the bark's texture, which was a good touch. There was something else, too. She ran her eyes carefully over the sculpture, taking in Mary's smooth hood, down-turned face, the drape of her sleeves from where she held the baby. Then Allie saw it. The statue was positioned in the exact place where light from outside streamed through the window and landed on the baby, creating the glowing effect of glory. Allie studied the window, trying to determine if the light always came in like that according to Genevieve's careful placement, or if it were only at this time in the day. In the end she couldn't really tell, with all those trees filtering the sunlight.

"Lovely day out, isn't it?" Genevieve asked, ignoring her own coughing fit and seemingly oblivious to the glow.

Allie nodded. "Quite nice, yes."

They sat, staring out the window. Trees were all they could see. Occasionally a bird sprang off a branch, setting free a brown or yellow leaf. Allie turned her head to watch Genevieve. Her eyes had a rheumy look: watery around the edges, the lids creased and sagging at the corners. The light in the dining room revealed more than the light in the sitting room; it showed liver spots and bruises.

"When do you usually work on your sculptures?" Allie asked.

"Hmm?" Genevieve pulled her gaze from the window. She lifted her teacup to her mouth and swallowed. "It's been a few weeks since I last worked on one."

Allie nodded and sipped her own tea victoriously. That made more sense, she thought. Genevieve didn't look strong enough to use woodworking tools or mix cement.

"My father used to whittle," the old woman said, staring into the trees. "He'd make balls and cubes and triangles while Mother read a story out loud. We had plenty of dice in the house, though Mother disapproved of card playing."

Allie smiled. Why does everyone assume that abstraction always follows representational art? Here was a homegrown example of Genevieve's people growing out of her father's whittled shapes. She would have to tell Jerry about this; he appreciated contemporary stories that fulfilled the old historical art patterns. He might even want to stop in and meet Genevieve, have a talk with her, write up an article for his fellow art historians to read.

A sound of tires crunching the gravel driveway brought both women to attention. Allie shook her head. For all her aging, the older woman had good hearing. Allie again wished that she'd have Genevieve's sharp wits when she was that age.

"That must be my son-in-law, Tom. He'll let himself in the door," Genevieve said, pushing her teacup toward the center of the table.

A car door slammed and they heard footsteps on the creaky porch. The door opened and a big male voice called in, "It's just me." He walked within, closing the door behind him.

Genevieve turned in her chair and said, "Come in, Tom. We're in the dining room."

Tom walked into the dining room and nodded his head at Allie before pulling up a chair. The whole room filled with the crisp, woodsy smell he carried in his thick graying hair and plaid lumberjack shirt. He had a bushy gray mustache and his cheeks were red. Allie guessed it was a permanent, weather worn red rather than the result of exertion.

"Howdy, ma'am. You must be the one who couldn't get through," he said, fidgeting with the teacup Genevieve had pushed away.

Allie smiled and extended her hand. "Allie Oxford. I appreciate you calling the county about the tree."

He squeezed her hand. "It was nothing. I'm Tom, married to her daughter, Carrie." He nodded at Genevieve. He let go of her hand and said, "They're out there now, cutting up the tree. The road should be clear in ten, twenty minutes."

"Wonderful," Allie said. She brushed off her pant legs and looked around the room. "I've had a lovely visit here with your mother-in-law. And her other, silent guests." She laughed, glancing at the statues.

Tom laughed, too. "Yes, the little people. They're always watching us, right, Ma?"

"Always." Genevieve nodded her head.

They fell silent and Allie studied Mary again. With the baby glowing in the window light, and the echoes of Genevieve's solemn *Always* running through her head, Allie again felt a little wary of the sculptures, as if they really were watching her. She had to take long breaths to slow her pulse. What must it be like to live among them, day in and day out? Did Genevieve ever flip a light switch and forget for one horrible second that all those people were her own wooden creations?

"Allie has a son in New York," Genevieve told Tom.

Tom raised his eyebrows. "Is that right? New York, huh?" He brushed his mustache with one hand. "Wow."

Allie smiled, wondering what Tom thought of when he thought of New York. "Wendell works at a hotel," she said.

"No kidding," Tom raised his eyebrows again. He nudged Genevieve's arm. "Well, you know all about that." He laughed, then explained to Allie, "This used to be Green Inn."

Allie nodded. "I saw the sign on the door."

Allie and Tom nodded together until Tom rubbed his mustache again and said, "New York. Do you get to visit often?"

She thought of the last time she had called Wendell and asked if it would be okay to fly in some day. He had made some excuse about his roommates always being around and how he wasn't feeling so hot lately and didn't think he was up to hitting the museums and galleries with her. Allie shook her head. "No, not often."

"Well, it's pretty far out there." He paused. "Is it the city—New York City—that we're talking about?"

As he asked that, Genevieve stood up, holding to the table's edge. She scraped back her chair and walked toward the sitting room.

Tom half-rose from his seat. "Can I get you something, Ma?"

Genevieve shook her head. "No, I'm just going to see what I can find for our guest before she leaves."

"Oh, good idea." He winked at Allie, who watched Genevieve disappear into the sitting room. She looked at Tom. "Can I ask you something?"

He nodded. "Sure."

She lowered her voice. "These statues. Does she really make these by herself?"

Tom chuckled. "Hard to believe, isn't it? Carrie and I sometimes take people over here just to have them look at them. Everyone is pretty amazed. It's too bad you won't be here at night. I rigged up the place so they're lit from below. It looks *spiritual*, Ma says, like God is right there among them."

Allie shivered, thinking of the mass of Israelites with shadows leaping up their faces.

Tom laughed. "Yep, it makes you shiver just thinking about it."

She smiled and braced against the table to push herself up. "It's been so kind of you and your mother-in-law to take me in like this."

"You know what they say about angels unawares." Tom laughed, standing up and pushing his chair out of Allie's way.

Allie didn't really know what they said about angels unawares, but she thought it meant she might be an angel. Now *that* was something Jerry would laugh at. Maybe she would tell him that next time he poked his head in her studio. She'd explain to him, face straight, that according to the latest findings she might very well be an angel, which meant that her painting was, well, perfect, all the colored stripes aligned to some heavenly order, reflecting the best of themselves in their neighboring stripes. She would need all the help she could get. Jerry wasn't too thrilled with her stripe paintings. He never said anything, had never pronounced *stripes* with that mild disdain, but Allie knew by the way he avoided talking about them. His silent disapproval meant more than she dared think about. It meant she might be past her prime. Maybe all her best work was behind her.

They walked into the sitting room. Genevieve had somehow maneuvered through the throng of Israelites, and was lifting a small figurine off a shelf. She turned it over in her hands and glanced at Tom. He moved as close to the shelf as he could get and leaned over, balancing himself on one of the cement hoods. He took the figurine from Genevieve.

"That's for you, Allie," Genevieve said, holding onto the shelf.

Tom handed over the figurine, and Allie looked at it, rubbing her thumb along the sanded wood. It was a boy in a robe. "I can't take this," she said.

"He's Joseph," Genevieve said. "He's wearing the robe his father gave him. He had many brothers." She swept her hand over the statues' heads. "But his father loved him the most."

Tom smiled. "When I was boy, that was one of my favorite stories. Joseph and his dreams. He was a dreamer, all right."

Genevieve slowly picked her way through the crowd. Tom stood nearby, holding out his hand now and then as if afraid she would fall.

The Joseph figure didn't have much expression on his face. Genevieve had etched zigzag designs into the robe. His arms were attached to his sides so that he looked stiff, as though standing at attention. She looked again. Or perhaps he was dreaming. Allie decided she'd have to dig out a Bible and look up the story. Dreaming about what? She said, "You really don't need to give me any gifts, after you invited me in and served tea..."

"You must take it," Genevieve said. "He'll remind you of your son."

Now she would really have to look up the story. Allie watched the old lady, more skeptical than ever over the soundness of her mind. Sometimes she said things that didn't quite make sense. But then, her own mother had done the same thing toward the end, and it hadn't meant a total loss of sanity. She clutched Joseph in both her hands. She would accept him, then, if it made Genevieve feel better. She would show Jerry, and then she would set it up in her studio or maybe on a bookshelf, and she would remember this odd collection of sculptures tucked away in the woods. More importantly, she would remember Genevieve. Maybe the stolid image of Genevieve chipping away at a piece of wood would be the stimulus that would lift Allie out of her rut, move past her paintings rife with stripes, strive for something more significant. Why should she freeze at the sense that she was past her prime, that all her work was for herself alone?

Tom and Genevieve saw Allie to the door, and she thanked them again as she stepped down the creaky porch steps. They waved as she got in her car and backed out of the driveway. She honked twice before turning out of sight into the trees.

The orange-vested construction workers were still clearing the road, moving between the chopped-up tree and a big truck. Allie pulled over and watched them, deciding to wait it out this time. She stared out the windshield until the trees and the construction men became blurry and Joseph appeared, reflected on the glass, superimposed over the fall colors. Now that she had it in her car, the Joseph figure *did* remind her of Wendell. Wendell the dreamer. She would surprise him with a visit soon, and give the figure to him as a gift. When was the last time she gave him a work of art? When was the last time she had given him anything, had overcome the barrier he had been building—ever so subtly—between them? It could jar him out of artistic paralysis, turn his life around.

She studied the reflection some more, not at all bothered by her stalled progress. She liked the shape of the reflection against the abstract autumn colors. The Wendell-figure, for all its woodenness, added life and interest to the composition. Could she paint it? If she did, she would have to lighten the reflection somehow. It looked too dark. The edges of the windshield framed the painting, but then Allie added the passenger window so it became a diptych. One large tree branch formed a strong diagonal, countered by the horizontal ditch-line and the vertical tree trunks. A good composition, but she knew it would need something more, something to add meaning. Then Allie blinked and everything came into high detail. She could see each bright leaf, shining like the golden moments of her past, still clinging to their branches but ready to fall and fade away. She could see how much pride she had taken in her past success; it had grown large, so that when it fell it stalled her progress as much as the tree blocked her car from continuing down the road. She could see the dark reflection of Joseph, who had become Wendell, and the darkness manifested her fears for his future. She could see her own eyes reflected in the window, and they too were darker than she expected.

A cold chill swept through her as she studied the reflection of her eyes. They looked dull, used up. No wonder she no longer put herself into the world of her paintings. She rubbed her throbbing knee as she thought dejectedly of what this painting really meant. She would have to paint it.

By now the construction workers were giving Allie the signal to move through.

Silver Medallions

Dad burned tires at night on the stone pile east of the cornfield. Dark smoke burned holes into the night, black holes that swallowed the stars. He took care to burn on quiet nights, but sometimes a light wind came up later and Sarah and I would open our bedroom curtains and watch as gray, semi-transparent sheets of smoke drifted across the moon as across a screen. One morning after a night of smoke, we went out in flip-flops and walked over the inky, flaky remains on the stone pile. As we made our way over the strange scars of the fore-night, we scared up a fat raccoon who scurried into the weeds that buttressed the fence.

Listening to the coon cry its high, sharp screeches, Sarah said, "Dad smoked out its home in the stone pile and killed its family. Did you see the rings on its tail and the mask around its face?"

I shrugged. "That's the way all raccoons look."

Sarah nodded gravely, her pale blue eyes serious and knowing. "Yes, but on *this* raccoon the rings represent life and death. A black ring for each death in the family and a brown ring for each new life. When the fat raccoon dies, its tail will turn all black. *And,* the mask around the eyes means this raccoon is wise and has seen much in the world, so much that it wishes it hadn't been born with eyes."

Sarah spoke this way. She read books, many more books by that young age than I have ever read, and I knew they told her things I would never know. Not only that, every morning she woke with remembered dreams. She wrote them down in her diary, and sometimes she told me about them. I always believed her, whatever she said.

I glanced at the fence where the raccoon had disappeared. I felt sorry for it. "Do you know the raccoon's name?"

Sarah nodded again. "The name is Mara because Mara means bitter."

We left the stone pile and continued walking down the dusty lane, dirt gathering between our toes as we counted the ladybugs and butterflies along the way. Sarah counted the spots on the ladybugs—two spots meant the ladybug was two years old. Six spots meant it was six years old. A white ladybug was older than its spots, and a very orange ladybug was sick, like a baby with jaundice. She called me to her side, beckoning me with her skinny, freckled arm as she hunched over a soybean plant, her pale hair falling to both sides of her face. I hunched over, and Sarah introduced me to a tiny red ladybug.

"Ooo, a cute baby bug."

"No, Kimmie, she's not a baby, she's a princess. This ladybug is beautiful and will rule the entire soybean field one day."

I looked across the wide expanse of the field, lush and green, each three-leafed canopy moving gently in a breeze, catching flashes of sunlight from the white-blue sky. A vast soybean kingdom with a ladybug princess was a fairy tale place, and I thought about that for a minute, in sheer awe. I was still young then, only nine, and didn't think beyond summer and warmth and beauty.

But Sarah, older, remembered winters, and her voice dropped into a shadowy whisper. "Even a beautiful princess will have a hard life. She will begin to be sad in just one or two months."

"Why? What could make her sad?" I asked, but Sarah would not tell me.

Instead, she said, "I wonder if ladybugs dream of flying far away, to other places where soybeans don't even exist."

We stood, squinting across the field to the line of trees that hid the house. Just before the line of trees stood two rows of black raspberry bushes, their prickly branches bearing little green leaves and hard green berries that would flush red and then soften into deep black, a black that would smear across our hands and mouths. I turned to Sarah, my mind on the fruit. "Do you think the black raspberries will be ripe soon?"

Sarah looked down. She was only two years older than me, but always much taller. She laughed quickly, imitating our mother, who laughed only in short bursts. "Kimmie, where did that come from?"

I shrugged and we walked back, our flip-flops popping against the gravel lane, our t-shirts billowing in the breeze, dragonflies zipping above our heads like tiny electric planes over a runway.

*

The next day Sarah received a silver invitation in the mail. A girlfriend was throwing a birthday party. All of Sarah's classmates had been invited, even the boys. On the afternoon of the party, Sarah stepped out of her room wearing a long aqua-colored sundress and shimmery lip-gloss. Her shiny, sun-bleached hair wrapped around itself in a tight bun. Sarah didn't look older than eleven, but her eleven was something more than most. More mature. She stood very straight and still in front of us, waiting to be looked at, a small smile on her lips. I hung over the back of a chair, staring at Sarah while our dad let out a long whistle. "Who's this pretty lady?"

Sarah blushed and laughed.

I watched from the kitchen window as Mom backed out of the garage in the slate gray minivan, Sarah buckled into the front passenger seat, staring straight ahead, her hands clasped in her lap. Mom's mouth was moving, but Sarah didn't appear to be listening; her smile was too distant. I thought of the ladybug princess, because Sarah looked like a princess, and I wondered again what could come to make her sad.

That night Sarah sat in bed reading a book. I stood in front of the bedroom mirror, studying my face: its full cheeks, reddish complexion, wide forehead. I pulled back my long dark-blond hair and tried to wrap it like Sarah had. Sarah looked up and laughed at my reflection. "What are you doing?"

I bit my lip and bunched my hair in a ball on top of my head. "Trying to look like you."

Sarah put down her book. "Why do you want to look like me?"

"You're pretty." I let go of my hair and sighed as it fell in front of my face.

"So are you."

I shook my head. Hair flew up in staticky wisps. "You're prettier." It would always be true, I knew. I knew, too, that she would try to persuade me otherwise.

Sarah scooted to the end of the bed and took a small box out of the top dresser drawer. She opened it and handed it to me.

I took it. "What's this?" I lifted out a wide silver bracelet inset with turquoise stones and silver medallions.

"I wore it to the party. Remember when Aunt Anne visited from New Mexico? She gave me this bracelet."

I slipped the bracelet around my wrist. It hung there, cool and heavy. I remembered the visit from our aunt. "She only gave me a book."

"She told me the sun medallion is for growth, the feather medallion is for creativity, the water bird medallion is for distant vision and wisdom."

"I didn't see you wearing it." I would have noticed that. I had her entire outfit memorized.

Sarah shrugged. "I had it in my dress pocket until I got to the party."

"How come?"

She shrugged again.

I raised my arm and watched the bracelet fall to my elbow.

Sarah said, "The bracelet has powers."

I stopped wiggling my arm.

"The longer you wear it the more beautiful you become." Sarah unhooked the bracelet from my arm and returned it to the box. "But its magic doesn't last forever. Once the magic runs out the medallions begin to rust and the turquoise stones turn into ebony. And your beauty begins to fade."

I stared into the mirror. I parted my hair and pulled it away from my face, vaguely recalling some fairy tale Sarah once read me.

"See," Sarah said, putting away the box, "it worked on you already."

I nodded slowly. Yes, I could see that. A glimmer of something I had seen in Sarah's face stared back at me. It was the knowing look. I practiced looking as if I knew an interesting secret, turning my head to the side, smiling a small smile.

When the lights were out and I was almost asleep, Sarah shook my arm. "Kimmie?"

"What?"

Sarah leaned close, and I could feel her hot breath against my ear. "The bracelet has another power too."

I shifted, pulling the blankets toward my side of the bed. I wanted to sleep.

Sarah continued, "It makes you feel like you're someplace else."

"Where?" I asked, yawning.

"Any place you dream of."

"It didn't take me anyplace."

"Then you must dream of home."

"Oh." I rolled onto my back and glanced at Sarah. She was staring at the dark light fixture.

"I dream of lots of places," she said. "Do you think I'll ever get to any of them, Kimmie?"

The question confused me. Or, rather, the fact that she had asked at all. My opinion had never mattered before, and I blinked, awake suddenly, remembering the magical bracelet. I tried to think of something to say, some assurance that Sarah would indeed fulfill her dreams, but I could only think of the ladybug princess, who would never leave her soybean field. I said, "There was the party today. That was getting away."

She sighed. "I came back, Kimmie. Besides, it wasn't a dream at all. It was like a party we might have here at home."

"Why do you always want to leave home?" I asked, yawning.

She remained silent for so long that I thought she had fallen asleep. I was almost asleep myself when she whispered, "I wasn't meant to live here. I was meant for bigger things."

*

She continued living with us. What choice did she have? She continued dreaming, too. That winter, on the first day of snow, the cows broke through the fence. Dad called for help. I was at the table, eating breakfast with Mom. Sarah was still upstairs.

"You'll have to be late for school today," Mom said. "Go get Sarah. Hurry up."

I flew up the stairs and into our bedroom. Sarah looked up from her diary, pen in hand, the bracelet from Aunt Anne on her arm. She grabbed at it when I came in, as if to hide it.

"Come on, Sarah, the cows are out!" I pulled her off the bed so fast that the pen and diary fell to the floor. She tried to yank her arm out of my hand, but I had a grip and wasn't letting go. Downstairs, I threw her coat at her, and we ran to the barn. Dad met us at the door, holding whips fashioned from yellowing rubber hoses which used to connect the cow udders to the milker.

Five cows stood in the field, sniffing the new snow. They itched the ground with their hooves and glanced up, the hair on their spines ruffled from excitement. Five beautiful, wild-with-freedom Holsteins, their black and white hides camouflaged against the black, snow-spotted earth. The scene called for a camera, a painter's easel, an image stretched across someone's living room wall. I thought they were the most beautiful things on earth. Dad, Mom, and I slowly slipped around the fence and began to circle the cows, Dad and I going one way, Mom going the other. Sarah stepped gingerly behind us, watching the cows. She had never liked them.

Dad told Sarah to stay where she was, near the fence. He told me to go behind and herd them forward. The cows watched me warily, huddling together as I neared them.

We were a square, slowly compressing. Dad stood in one corner. Sarah huddled in the other corner, her nose red from the cold air, her posture too thin, like a post for the cows to run past. Mom, arms outstretched, waved her whip as she took the third corner, and I stood behind the cows. They stirred uneasily, shifting their attention from one corner to the next, immense energy trembling behind the nervous twitch of each movement.

Dad called out, "Kimmie, push them in. Push them in."

I rushed forward, arms at full wingspan and slapped the first cow I came to with my whip. This drew startled moos and the rolling of big cow eyes. And then they put their heads down and charged toward Dad's side. I ran toward him as he steered them around. Together we drove them the other direction. The lead cow had her nose across the fence border but she bucked back, veered toward Dad, did an about-face and charged at Sarah.

Sarah yelped and tried to stand in the way, but the first cow brushed past—"Don't let them get by! Hit them! Turn 'em around!"—and so did the second cow, but Sarah kicked the third and pounded into its face with her whip. The slap of rubber against bone bounced as sound off the frozen ground. The cow shook its head, confused, then turned and broad-sided the other two. It drove them through the hole in the fence, and there they stopped running and stood sniffing the familiar ground. They walked slowly to the feed bin. The two that got away stood still, staring after the other three cows. It only took a small dose of Mom's persuasion to herd them into the yard as well. Dad fixed the fence while Sarah and I stood nearby, sniffing because our noses were running from the cold.

"You did good," Dad said, wiping his own nose with the back of his glove.

Sarah sniffed and looked away. "I guess." She looked embarrassed, and maybe a little proud of Dad's compliment.

"Yes!" I agreed, still excited. "Look at them eat."

"Like nothing happened," Sarah added.

"Stupid beasts," Dad said, standing up, watching the cows.

Sarah sniffed, nodding. We watched them lick up the haylage, pushing the feed away with their noses, then stretching their tongues to get it back. *Stupid beasts*, Dad always called them. But they had weight and they had stubborn wills and when they wanted to move, they could go places.

When Dad walked away, I said, "Sorry I pulled you out of the house like that." I laughed a little. "Did you have another dream last night?"

Sarah nodded. "It wasn't anything great. Just another dream."

I stared at her. Whenever I asked, she always told me her dreams, each magical detail fantastical to me, like something pulled from a beautiful fairy tale.

She cleared her throat and began telling, but not with her normal confidence. "I dreamed of a fire with no smoke. From out of the fire flew birds of all colors. A red one landed on my shoulder, and it whispered me directions to a city far away."

I noticed she had her hand in her coat pocket, and I thought I could see the outline of the bracelet inside her pocket. She hadn't had time to take it off.

Sarah continued, "I couldn't go, for some reason. I woke up."

"What?" I had been watching the cows, who were still eating. I thought I hadn't heard right. "What did you say?"

"I woke up. That was the end of the dream." She sniffed, and this time I imagined it wasn't from the cold.

I looked closely at my sister, and somehow, despite the magical bracelet in her pocket, despite the glow of pride born from chasing the cows into the yard, she looked broken. This would be the dream that came true. And when her gaze met mine, I was the one with the sad, knowing look in my eyes, and she was the one looking to me for answers.

I didn't have the answers, then. I was only a kid. Sarah grew up and experienced what might be called a typical teenage rebellion, except when it came to Sarah nothing was typical. She retreated even further into the mystical world she had created among her books, her diary, and her dreams. She no longer confided in me concerning these things. On a summer night, one calm and ringing with insect song, she tried to run away. Her diary entry from the night before revealed that she had an intricate plan, beginning with a bus ride to Chicago. She called it her "flight for life." She never made it to the big city. She didn't even get on the bus.

Shouldering a duffel bag, walking along our lonely country road on a moonlit night, Sarah snagged a ride from a man in a red Ford pickup. Whether this man was a stranger to her, or someone she had relied on as part of her escape plan, we still don't know. The man was drunk. Two miles from our house, the pickup veered into the path of an oncoming semi, killing both the driver and Sarah in one quick snap. I was fourteen; she was sixteen.

Four years later, the day before I left for college, I walked slowly down the lane between the tall walls of corn and the dense fields of soybeans. The ladybugs were thick that year, and I remembered Sarah's story of the sad ladybug princess. She had been that princess. Her medallion bracelet wrung my wrist. I had found it in the back of our closet a week earlier, when I was packing for college. I had taken to wearing it because it reminded me of her and of the magic that had died when she died. The hot sun loomed directly overhead, reflected brightly off the medallions as I let the band slide up and down my arm. A dragonfly zipped around my head and landed briefly on the bracelet. I held my breath, transfixed by its body's iridescent blue shimmer and the sheerness of its see-through wings. It zipped into the tall corn and was gone, but that moment of raw beauty and clarity stung me the next day as I drove away from the farm, leaving for the first time to live somewhere else. This had been Sarah's dream, and I was fulfilling it for her. I wanted to call her back, just for a moment, so I could tell her how much she still meant to me, that remembering her quiet composure brought me through anxious moments of my life. I wanted her to know how the cadences of her natural speech inspired the words I struggled to arrange into poetry, and how those poems won my way to a good school.

I wanted to tell Sarah she had one thing wrong that morning we saw the raccoon scurry from the smoking burn pile. She had said the mask around the raccoon's eyes meant the animal was wise and had seen many things that would make it wish it hadn't been born with eyes. I have seen many things, and I wish some of them had not happened, but I am glad for knowing them. They have made me better, somehow. It is not a mask, really, but a lens that bends all things, the good and the bad, so they become one continuing spectrum of wisdom and grace.

Portrayal

I itched to paint the smooth color of Leap's dark skin. He blended well in the warm brown atmosphere of Habbie's Spirits, which was a bar, a bar which I wanted to leave. I also wanted to stay and memorize every mahogany table and chair, every oak beam, every burnt umber shadow. Light gleamed off the glasses and bottles, giving a sparkling, enchanting effect. Gray wisps swirling up from the smokers' cigarettes reminded me of genii smoke; three wishes granted, but be careful what you wish for because it might come true. Two musicians in the corner strummed their guitars and hummed.

I wished I could split in half like a tree struck by lightning—half Lindsay the Good, half Lindsay the Temptress. Good Lindsay would be in my dorm room, saying her prayers. The other half could remain here, look deep into Leap's dark eyes, stare my way into his heart.

Of course, a tree struck by lightning is dead.

"Your necklace is burning," he said. His gaze was a sponge, soaking me up from across the table. His skin shone more the longer he looked at me.

I brought my hand to my throat, fingered the gold necklace he had given me.

"You moved." He sighed and drank his beer.

I tried to remember how I had been sitting. "Is this right?" I looked at the light fixture hanging above me, shaped like a Japanese lantern and paned with frosted, yellow-tinted glass. The fixture's structure was bronze, a little shinier and more angled than Leap's skin, but a very similar color.

"No," Leap said. "You won't get it again. It was a once in a lifetime event."

He said things like that. Once in a lifetime event. Took my breath completely away. Everyone else will die, but I'll live forever. He took everything to its extreme, especially his own painting. Each new painting was by far his best one yet. By default, it was also the best painting in the class; Leap had the most talent. All of us around the table at Habbie's Spirits were aware of it, and we accepted it. Some of the other girls called me lucky because I was his girl. Already, I was *Leap's girl*, though I wasn't completely sure of it myself. The necklace helped convince me, as did our nighttime rendezvous in the painting studio.

I looked down from the fixture, which cast warm light on his shiny black hair, spilled it over his cheekbones and across the slightly concave skin to his jaw, which, when his mouth opened wide, looked like a delicate hinge stretched with a thin layer of flesh. The light pooled off his bangs, running a yellow streak down his nose, which was wide at the nostrils. His lips—I licked my own lips and felt my face heat up—were barely there, just a smooth transition from honey brown to a pink brown of the same value.

In black and white, the lips were invisible, a crease where they came together. I knew because I had drawn him before. Several times before. If art thrives on obsession, then Leap was my obsession.

When Leap finished his beer, we danced. I didn't know how to dance, and I didn't want to learn, but Leap came around the table and put his hands on my shoulders, his thumbs kneading into my muscles.

"Come on," he said, running his hands down my arms, pulling back my chair.

To resist Leap was to resist a river's strong undertow. I let him pull me to the floor, though I already felt awkward, as if all the weight in my body had collected in my arms and legs. I had grown up believing dancing was wrong, though I hadn't learned why until one of my friends explained that my parents thought dancing led directly to sex.

It might be true, I thought, as Leap's arms locked around me. He rested his cheek against mine and I inhaled a scent I had come to know—sweet like caramel and musky like earth after slow rain. Maybe if I tried to forget about feet and hands, if I just closed my eyes and let myself fall into Leap, I could get over the stiffness in my legs. The singer was a little off-key, but the mood of the song was very slow and sensual, and I realized that Leap was barely moving, just swaying a little, humming the tune, his hums a low drone, the sound of thumbs tapping on the table while your ear is pressed to the tabletop.

If this was dancing, then we had danced before, in a dark, empty studio, standing on the model's stand, moonlight from the high windows touching the crowns of our heads. We were working late on our still life drawings. That was only three or four weeks ago, but I seemed so young then. I had jumped onto the model's stand and draped myself with a satiny cloth, declaring myself a princess. "A princess of what," he asked, and then he stopped smiling and turned off the lights in the studio. I must have moved, but he told me to stop. "Don't move one muscle." Those were his exact words. I tried not to, though I couldn't help thinking that my heart was a muscle, and it was pounding harder than before. I realized what he was doing: he found in me a subject, and he stared at me the way he studied a row of glass bottles, a collection of pottery, the sleek bone-white bust sitting on a table to my right. And then he was right there, in the dark, holding me.

I clung to him on the dance floor in Habbie's Spirits as I had in the studio that first night. Closing my eyes, I thought of beautiful things—the Monet posters on the studio walls, the da Vinci drawings, *myself* in Leap's painting. I wore a yellow dress and a satin cloth hung from my arms. My head tilted up toward a spotlight.

The song ended and Leap pulled away, his hands squeezing my upper arms. "Were you even listening to me?"

I blinked. "Your humming?"

He laughed. "I said you're a pretty good dancer." "Really?"

"Really." He grabbed my arm and led me back to the table. He caught a waitress with the other hand. "Beer please."

She flicked her eyes between me and Leap. "Two beers coming up."

Leap raised his eyebrows at me. "Thanks," he said, and the waitress left.

We sat down and stared at each other. "Tell me exactly what you're thinking," he said.

I wished I had his tongue; his was brazen enough to tell the whole truth. I had a weak tongue and would never say what I wanted. I wanted to kiss him. Instead, I said, "I was thinking of you at church. You know, the pose I wanted to paint you in." It was semi-true. I had wanted to kiss him in church, too.

He laughed. "You think too much about church."

The drinks came and I stared at the brown bottle set in front of me. I could see how I would paint it, with yellow-white highlights curving around the neck, and dark black-browns settling toward the bottom, weighing it down. Then I blinked and saw it for what it really was—a distraction. Turning my attention back to Leap, I said, "We could still do it, you know. I'd have enough time to make that painting. I could get permission from the pastor and you could pose two or three times for me."

He shook his head. "I don't want to be portrayed that way."

"You said it was beautiful."

He had said it was beautiful. When I took him to church with me one Sunday morning, he slipped into the bench beside a window, and the sunlight poured into the sanctuary as the pianist began her prelude. Leap turned his head slowly to admire the light, and something outside caught his eye—maybe a latecomer in the parking lot, maybe a bird—but that was when I saw the image I wanted to paint. Because he was closer to the window than me, I saw his dark features even darker in contrast to the bright light surrounding his head like a sunburst. I imagined myself three benches ahead, looking back at Leap looking out the window. Looking at a man finding something familiar in an unfamiliar setting.

Leap drank some of his beer and put it down again. "That place was everything I'm not. I only went because you asked me so sweetly."

I wrapped my hand around the cold beer bottle, wiping away condensation with my thumb. This was what I struggled with—this pull between Leap's world and mine. Or was it my old world and my new world? Or was it no world at all, but just a place I fell into? I let go of the bottle and looked away, hiding my hands in my lap.

"What?" Leap asked. "You're going to sulk now? You need to loosen up. We're here to have fun." He reached over and pushed the bottle closer to me. "Drink."

"I don't drink."

The guitarists ended their song, and the other people at the bar seemed to all stop talking at the same time. We heard the clink of glasses as a bartender set them out. It was one of those uncomfortable silences that happens in public places sometimes, but Leap smiled and leaned over. "Look what you did," he whispered.

I tried to glare at him, but I couldn't keep from smiling. The music and talking started up again. We stared at each other. It was something we had a habit of doing, and it unnerved me. I blinked and tried to reverse the feeling. "Tell me exactly what you're thinking," I said.

Leap grinned. "One of my old girls used to paint herself for me."

"What?"

"She undressed and painted on her body. It was really quite lovely." He breathed in deeply, staring somewhere into the past. "A private art performance."

I didn't know what to do with that sort of information.

"What happened to her?" I asked.

"Oh, I don't know," Leap said, loud and gusty, like people do when they're tired of talking. "She graduated, I think." He looked at the musicians. "You want to dance again?"

I didn't, but I said I did. When I was back in his arms, swaying gently to the music, I told myself I really did want to dance. An alarm, a voice, a pull from deep inside my head warned me I was headed down the wrong path. Pretty soon I'd be one of his old girls. Maybe he painted portraits of all of them, a record of sorts, something he could gloat over later. He probably had them lined up in his room in Chicago, some of them nude. Tallies on the wall. I would look like a prude next to them, a silly, naive girl who fell for Leap with hardly any persuasion. He would tell his next girl I was "easy."

"Why are you hanging on so tight?" Leap asked, breathing into my ear.

I loosened my grip, and shrugged. "Was I?"

He chuckled. "Like it was the end of the world."

I wished it was the end of the world. I could stop this shifting from one Lindsay to another. I could finally figure out where I belonged, and I'd have eternity to do so.

Leap led me to the door.

"What are you doing?" I asked.

"Leaving."

"Why?" I glanced back at the bar, the nine or ten couples on the dance floor, the guys at the counter telling jokes and drinking too much, the beautiful lights, all the beautiful browns.

He opened the door and pulled me outside. Wind blew into our faces, sending goosebumps up my arms. The night smelled like the river, dirty from recent rains and rotten from waterlogged wood. He pulled me down the cracked sidewalk toward a bench smothered in an employment agency advertisement. The streetlight above the bench dimmed as we sat down, then burned bright again.

"Why did we leave?" I asked again, shivering.

Leap smiled and pulled a small sketchbook from his back pocket. The brown paper cover was bent and worn at the edges. He opened it to an empty page and dug a stubby pencil from a different pocket. "Put your chin up."

I put my chin up. "You're going to draw me? Out here?"

He started a loose sketch. "There's something different about you tonight. My painting makes you seem holy, almost like you're a— Tonight you seem more human. Insecure and wild. Turn your face to the road."

So he liked me insecure and wild.

I turned my face toward Leap and snatched the sketchbook from his hands.

"Hey!"

I took the pencil, too, and held it over the paper, such a familiar position that my fingers nearly began sketching the moment my eyes met his. But I held my hand still as I studied his face, his black eyes, the deep shadows in his ears, beneath his nose, under his chin. A fly buzzed in front of his face, and he shooed it away with a hand, never losing eye contact with me. He seemed mesmerized.

I carved a smooth line across the page. Then I drew another line—the beginning of his eye socket.

I kept drawing, faster now, driven by some force. If I drew, then I wouldn't be expected to speak. If I drew, maybe I wouldn't even hear the voices in my head, telling me I should go back to my dorm, go far, far away from Leap. I'd be lost in the marks on that small piece of paper, lit by the cold streetlight above us.

The wind gusted, pulling my hair around my face, blowing the smell of salty French fries and bursts of laughter from Habbie's Spirits. Leap looked over my shoulder toward the bar. I drew his eyes like that, looking beyond the viewer.

The wind, bar noises, and passing cars flooded the air with so much sound that talking seemed impossible. After a while I stopped drawing and looked at what I had done. It was not a pretty picture, and definitely not my best attempt at getting the proportions right: one eye socket higher than the other, the gap between his nose and mouth too large and dark, the ears crooked, the chin pointy. I sighed, put the pencil back in the book's crease, and handed it to Leap. He took it and studied the picture.

"Your best yet," he said.

I turned to look at Habbie's Spirits. Warm light glowed through the windows; the sign on the front shone a cheerful neon white. Someone on the other end of our table would buy a round of shots for everyone. The band would strike up a slow, romantic tune, and couples would rise into each other's arms to sway to the music.

"Let's go back," Leap said, closer to me, his hand covering mine on the back of the bench.

"I'm not going back," I said.

Leap put his hands on my shoulders, so gently they tingled. I felt his hot mouth against my neck, and even though the wind still pulled all around us, the heat burned into my skin and up and down my body. I closed my eyes and concentrated so hard on being still that I could feel the heave of my chest and the pump of blood in my head. He whispered, "I meant back to my room."

I turned my head slowly until our noses were touching. I licked my lips and stared at Leap, his eyes so near they looked like perfect drops of ink in a white pool, framed by individual eyelashes, tapered to a point. When he blinked, it was in slow motion, a grand, sweeping movement that filled my vision. There was no other place, no past, no future. I held my breath.

Leap dropped his head and sighed. He let go and sat back on the bench. Wind blew his bangs across his forehead. Looking up into the dark sky, he said, "You're beautiful, Lindsay."

I watched him. He looked cool again, perfectly in control—a man sitting comfortably on a bench, one arm draped over the back, one ankle resting on his knee. He could be anybody, even a stranger. He wasn't the face I drew. I didn't even know whose face that was, except that it was wrong. If only he would throw it away.

My gaze rose to the streetlight, and higher to the moon. I squinted at its thick, white crescent, and it began to wave in my vision, reminiscent of the satin cloth I clung to in the studio as I posed for Leap. Somewhere, in another dimension, I heard him stand up and walk away, his feet cracking a branch on the sidewalk. It could just as well have been me walking away. It meant the same thing.

I sat there in the cool night air, thinking about his painting. Beneath the rag Leap covered his painting with, I shone out of the darkness, mysterious and mystical as a moon, barefoot and golden, gazing. He said I was beautiful. He was wrong. Me, I was only searching for something beautiful.

Craft Day

A group of women sit in a living room, crafting and chatting, occasionally casting glances out the large picture window at the leaden clouds lowering themselves over the dry stubble in the field across the road.

"Looks like snow," one says, snipping a thread.

"Wouldn't it be nice," says another, "to have a white Thanksgiving?"

The lady of the house, a tall woman who wears her hair and her long skirt the same way her great-grandma might have worn them, makes a harsh noise in the back of her throat. "It'd be nice to have a warm Thanksgiving." She pokes her needle in and out of her cross-stitch.

"Oh, but Laura, think of that fresh white coat over the ground, how pretty it is," insists Clara, the young woman who wants snow on Thanksgiving. She is decorating a curtain for her daughter's room, stitching brightly-colored buttons onto a length of pale yellow material.

Laura continues cross-stitching, following some pattern in her head. "Snow might look pretty, but it's all a cover-up. When it comes time to feed the cows and calves, I'd like to see you muck your way through that snowy barnyard." She nods her head in the direction of the barn.

Clara, determined to solicit support for her beliefs, turns to the woman next to her, the only one not stitching or knitting something, and the only one wearing jeans instead of skirts. "Jess, you know what I'm talking about, don't you? You're an artist. You appreciate the first snow for what it is."

Jess, her pencil paused above the sketchbook on her lap, smiles. "I do like the first snow."

"See!" exclaims Clara.

The women chuckle, and Jess laughs outright as Laura waggles a stern finger at her. "You just be quiet now, or I'll get up and sit somewhere else."

Jess looks down at her drawing. Noble and queenly, viewed from the side, Laura sits in the sketch, her large hands poised over the oval cross-stitch frame. The self-possession of the woman, a real quality that Jess admires in her, shows through the lines and shading. All eyes in the room turn toward the artist, and, as if the sketch has stolen from Jess the very thing she most wants to portray, a hot blush burns her face.

Clara, who befriended Jess the first day she and her husband joined their church, says warmly, "You certainly are amazing at drawing. Where did you learn to do that?"

Jess shrugs. "My father taught me to draw. And then I practiced a lot."

A hush falls over the women. The youngest of them, one of Laura's daughters, asks, "Was your father an artist, too?"

Laura sends her daughter a reproachful look, and the rest of the women pretend to be absorbed in their work. They know that Jess' father had a questionable history—a series of bankruptcies, drugs, divorce. Though Jess joined their church a few months ago as new wife to a respectable Christian young man, the stories of her bringing-up still circulated around their dinner tables. They shook their heads sorrowfully over the scalloped potatoes. In benevolent tones, they remarked how kind she seemed. Spooning up the buttered peas, someone raised her eyebrows and said that there was good reason for her to be so quiet.

Studying her drawing, the dark, sinuous lines slashed against the white paper, Jess answers, "Yes, in his own way."

Laura changes the subject to cooking, but in the backs of their minds, the women wonder in what way Jess' father had been *artistic*.

His artistry, in fact, was one of his good talents turned sour. Trained in advertisement, he shot out of school as an ambitious young man, ready to support his lovely new wife and the family they planned. But, when Jess was born, and health complications brought envelope after envelope of hospital bills, the advertising business proved not lucrative enough. He ventured on a side business, forging lesser-known works of famous artists, and in this he prospered for many years. Jess' earliest memory of her father was of him bent over a print, examining it with his magnifying glass. The light of the work lamp made his yellow hair shine like gold. Jess thought of him as a type of Midas, touching paper or canvas and magically transforming it.

When her parents divorced, Jess considered her dad's studio apartment a secret world, a world he shared with her during designated visits. He introduced her to the weights of art pencils, the nap on paper, the vanishing points of perspective drawing. She didn't know, then, that he wasn't honest. That he was master of secret ceremonies conducted away from her mother's watchful eye. Even when she did find out, when, after he went to jail and Jess learned from middle school classmates that her father was a drug addict and a criminal, Jess couldn't translate that god-like being into something less. Nor could she look at his artwork and assign it to some other maker, someone more upright and honest.

As she draws her portrait, deepening the shadows beneath the eyes, she senses the ladies' disapproval of her father's lifestyle. Under all their talk about pumpkin pie and green bean casseroles she trips on their incredulity over how Jess can speak of her father so casually. Well, her relationship with her father was *not* casual. Worshipful, fearful, respectful, yes, but not casual, not like the other daughters and fathers she had observed. The difference was plain. Now, as an adult, Jess carries a revered mental image of him. Revered. Definitely not casual. In her memory, he smiles tenderly at her. His charcoal sketch of her, lively and accurate, hangs beside him on the yellow wall. She has that same sketch in her possession, in a briefcase beneath her bed. When she needs reassurance that her father had loved her, she takes it out and looks at it. "I drew you, and here you are," he says, pleased as she imagines God was following his creation of Adam.

Isn't art the act of creation, after all? As God speaks the world into existence, so the artist extracts her own world from an empty place. Jess watches Laura's needle weave expertly in and out of the canvas, a green vine rising where there had been nothing. An emerging excitement causes Jess to shiver, and she wonders at her reaction. It has been a long time since she watched another artist at work. When she watched her dad draw, time and place seemed to cease. Those lines that stand for trees in the distance, the grass matted down in the foreground where the cows had trodden: she could smell the sweet clover, feel the hot breeze lift the hair from her damp forehead, hear a fly buzz around her head, though all the time she was in her father's stale studio, sitting on a black padded stool whose stuffing seeped out the cracks.

While he drew he would tell her bits of wisdom. Something he said about drawing people pulls on the corner of Jess' brain, retreats. Pulls, retreats. What is it?

The vine grows faster under Laura's needle, its tendrils curling at the ends, the main stalks twisting up strong and supple. The clicks of knitting needles in the room accelerate into a definite beat, and the ladies' voices become a sort of song, high-pitched and varied. Primal. Jess begins to feel lightheaded, as if in a dream from which she can't awaken.

She remembers the day she first feared her father. He talked bitterly about her mother, using vulgar words she didn't even know the meaning of but which came out soaked in vinegar. He ripped his drawings off his desk and tore them into little pieces. Jess crept into the kitchen where the phone was. She called her mother, whispering, and asked her to pick her up. Safe at home, her fear and hatred slipped away, and she forgave him everything. She forgave him because, except for this one exception, he guided his pencils so carefully and lovingly across the paper, creating beautiful little worlds Jess could step into. He was her father, and she loved him.

Once, he drew a woman similar to the one in the drawing on Jess' lap, except his woman was from the tropics, dark and clad in flowers and grass. But just as stately. Just as superior. Jess had drawn back in alarm at the sight of the woman that day. Those awful, large flowers at her shoulder and in her hair did nothing to soften the attention her large eyes and tight-set mouth commanded. Her father laughed at her reaction, but he hid the picture for the rest of the visit. The next time Jess visited him he showed her the finalized drawing, matted and framed. This time, Jess breathed easier in her presence. The dark, imposing woman was changed. Subtle shadows stole the raw power that had frightened Jess before. The delicately-drawn background of island trees and birds provided her a kingdom to command, absorbed the power that had previously asserted itself over the viewer. Jess admired her father for being able to rule even his strongest creations.

But this woman on Jess' lap is not finished. In the midst of her own act of creation, Jess had created something that is now taking over and creating itself. No longer a portrait of Laura, the old-fashioned, sharp-witted woman in the doily-draped armchair. No longer she who has now uncrossed her legs and is relating a funny story about her first Thanksgiving dinner, this woman has the bone structure of a goddess, the gaze of a queen, the authority of an angel. Moisture begins to collect under Jess' collar. Her pencil becomes slippery. She grips it tighter, whitening her thumbnail. Beneath the graphite the woman rises from the paper as if to climb out and breathe and take control, using her needle and thread as a scepter. She sits as if her chair is an extension of herself. She stitches as if stitching her own skin. She wears clothes as if they don't exist. If she talks—but no, she won't talk.

Jess moves the graphite tip back to the woman's lips, wavers, and lets the pencil drop into her bag. She rises abruptly, asks Laura the location of the bathroom, and sets the sketchbook, opened, on her chair.

The bathroom smells of work clothes and fruity shampoo. The toilet seat feels cool, and upon closer examination of the small window, a draft flutters the edge of the antique lace curtains. The water from the faucet takes a long time to warm up, and Jess lets the cool stream run over her hands as she studies her face in the mirror. The mirrored image belongs to someone who shies from self-examination. When she does examine, she never lives up to the expectations of those like the woman in her sketchbook. Her hair, thick and chin-length, hangs gracelessly and her bangs are cut crooked. Her glasses, too, sit crooked on her nose. Or does it only look that way because of the bangs? Jess tilts her head this way, then that. It doesn't matter. Her shirt hangs crooked, as well, the collar points curling up. She dries her fingers and palms on a hand-edged towel, and then tries to smooth down her collar, but to no avail. So be it, she thinks. She isn't cut out to be one of the quaint and lovely mothers in the other room, their skirts falling in graceful folds around their ankles, their long hair done up in braids and tiny bobby pins. Even Clara, with all her loud friendliness, has her black-heeled boots shined and her accessories matched.

The doorknob feels cool to the touch and Jess gives a backward glance at the fluttering lace curtain. Outside the window, a few flakes of snow drift across the gray sky.

"So much for my warm Thanksgiving," Laura is saying as Jess slips into her chair, propping the sketchbook on her lap.

Jess picks up her eraser, but the woman she wants to diminish seems to tell her to lay it down again. She obeys.

Clara leans over and says, "I told Laura she ought to keep this drawing and frame it. It's so well done!"

Laura looks up. "Yes, Jess. Unless you have other plans for it."

Suddenly, Jess remembers what her father said about drawing other people. "They are real—these people in the paper. But they aren't the same as anyone else. No matter how well you copy a face, it's still never the same face." He had been discussing a portrait Jess had drawn of him. She remembered it as fairly accurate but lacking the inner fire that defined her father. Jess compares her drawing to the real Laura. The real Laura, glancing expectantly at Jess, isn't this woman on the paper. The real Laura has a kind heart, for which Jess is grateful. The woman on the paper doesn't have a heart. Jess feels cold control brace her drawing hand. She no longer feels the heat of oppression or the wildness of creation. Her drawing, which surprised her when it became goddess-like, now retreats humbly back into the paper. Jess notices that the fine line of thread stretching from the needle to the canvas is disconnected in the middle, and the woman in her drawing sits on nothing but an outline of a chair, as though she lacks foundations. Even the oval cross-stitch frame, angled so the viewer can see a little of the stitching, has an air of incompleteness compared to the woman herself.

Jess leans over the page and says, "Let me finish it first."

She draws, and, later, as she names the painting *Someone Else,* scrawling this title in small print on the bottom right, another piece of paper comes to mind. Her father wrote her a letter from a detox center three days before he died. His handwriting, usually strong and assured like the lines in his drawings, now wavered and fluctuated across the single page. The message of the letter, in contrast, revealed a determined mind. "Remember me," he wrote, "as someone else. Don't think of me as the father who did you wrong. Never let bitterness darken your heart. It will destroy you. It will destroy all you do. I write from experience."

Jess responded immediately with her own letter, assuring her father that she loved him, that what he had done didn't matter to her. It arrived too late. Her father never read it. She keeps his final letter in the briefcase with his sketch of her, and when she reads it, often *only* while she reads it, she thinks of him as he *was*, not as the god who called his art into being. More than an artist, he was a man, as broken and weak as the handwriting in his letter.

How strange. The way this incomplete drawing had the power to keep her cowered until she mastered it, but her father's power to cower her fell apart in his own final weakness, just at the moment that she gained the strength to see him as he was.

The others are packing up their cross-stitches, dropping their skeins of yarn into their canvas workbags, and commenting on the snow, which is coming down much faster now. They gather around Laura's cross-stitch. Jess notices the vine has grown to be beautiful, and now some stitched letters of a Bible verse stabilize its presence on the canvas. She finishes her drawing as the last of the crafters leave, and Laura and her daughters bend here and there, straightening up the room. She detaches the page from the sketchbook and hands it to Laura without speaking. She wonders if Laura will like it, but she is not anxious. She has done her best. Laura thanks her and examines it at arm's length.

"You know," she says, "I don't think I look quite that good in real life."

Jess smiles. "Someone once told me that a good drawing contains both truth and falsehood." She gazes past the drawing and into the white, blowing snowstorm outside. "Just like real life."

Master of Light

You've just graduated with an art degree from a local college in Wisconsin and you're emailing a Reformed Baptist seminarian in California. Your mom thinks you'll make a great pastor's wife and your dad thinks you should have been out of the house four years ago. They've sold their milking cows, which had sentimental value to you, and replaced them with an idiot pack of steer who look dirty and completely unaware that the only reason they exist is to be killed and eaten. As you despair over the changes that life has dealt you the dairy farmer down the road puts out a marriage proposal. His kind, smiling face beams down on you like the man all tattered and torn who kisses the maiden all forlorn, and you take his hand in matrimony. Your husband decides to triple the size of his herd and build a new milking parlor and hire Mexican farm hands. One of the Mexicans gets kicked in the head and is never the same again, and all of a sudden you're buried under debt and a lawsuit. Your husband sells the corporation and moves you and your three-year-old daughter to a fourth-story apartment in Green Bay so he can work at his uncle's paper factory and take night classes to become a missionary. You buy sketchbooks, one for every month, and fill them with drawings of your childhood. More than a hobby or halfhearted interest, this becomes a necessary part of life, on par with cooking meals and saying grace.

The more you draw your own little sketches the more you crave more art, more beauty, more escape from the everyday dusting and laundry. After you find out you're pregnant again you buckle your daughter into her car seat and drive to the mall where someone somehow stuck a Kinkade art gallery between the pretzel counter and the pet store. Your daughter wriggles her hand out of yours and says, "Mommy, Mommy, look at the fish!" pressing her lips and sweaty hands smack against the pet store window, but you're here on a mission and you simply say, "The fish are sleeping, Sarah. Say 'nighty-night' and come into this pretty room with me." Once you're inside and surrounded by gold-framed Thomas Kinkade paintings, each lit from above by a small yellow light to create a serene and contemplative ambiance, Sarah shouts at the top of her lungs, "Thomas Kinkade!" but you don't feel at all guilty telling her the fish can hear everything in this room, which is why this room is always so quiet—and you stress the word *quiet.*

The paintings invite you into their world, and you think how easy it must be to walk along the stony banks of that sparkling blue river and rest beneath that pink-leaved tree before ambling through the white arbor to the stately brick mansion surrounded by evergreens, glowing from the inside with that famous Kinkade glow. You think you see your husband through the window, carving a turkey at the dining room table. You breathe the name of the painting, "Beside Still Waters," and Sarah punches your leg and says, "Shhhh!" loudly.

The gallery worker walks up to you, her hands clasped behind her back, and, though you anticipate a scold, she smiles. "Have you seen *Evening Majesty* yet?"

She leads you to the back room and invites you to turn the light dial. This shows the luminosity of Kinkade paintings, the gallery worker explains. As you slowly turn the dial from bright to dim, you watch the mountain-cabin scene transform from majestic and calm to holy and mysterious. You keep your hand on the dial, turning it back and forth at different speeds, finally turning it so slowly you think you're watching the sun set inside the painting. Sarah scatters into each corner of the room and whispers to the walls, "I love you, I love you."

After you tuck Sarah into bed and curl your legs into the arm chair you pick up the nearest magazine, *Hoard's Dairyman*, and read about the latest ways to prevent mastitis in cows while you wait for your husband to come home. You turn on a hymns instrumental album to drown out the football game in the apartment below. You hear the key in the lock during "The Old Rugged Cross," and when your husband walks in you find him entirely handsome, though you would never have guessed he'd wear penny loafers after all those years in work boots. You hum to the music as he leans down and kisses you. You've learned to hum while you're kissing because it vibrates inside both your mouths, like he and you are one musical instrument.

"I talked to Dr. Whiting," he says, hanging up his coat. "There's an opportunity for missions in the Philippines this coming summer. He thought we should take it."

You close your magazine and place it at the very center of your coffee table, thinking about the stack of *Hoard's Dairyman* that occupies the very center of your mother's coffee table. The Philippines is not a country you considered becoming a missionary in, and besides, you were expecting to spend the next summer here, in this apartment, waiting. And all at once you see it, that waiting has become your life, and you know it will take some serious adjustment before you become a doer instead of a waiter. With all this on your mind, and the Kinkade paintings still absorbed into your brain (their haunting, golden windows and winding paths will even swim through your dreams for several nights in a row) you decide you will wait to tell your husband about the baby.

When you do tell him, early one morning a few days later, while he is sitting on the side of your bed, pulling on his socks, he doesn't yell and pick you up and twirl you around like the day you told him about Sarah. So you say, "Late July, the doctor said. I have another appointment in a few weeks. Are you okay, Mark? You don't look so hot."

Mark doesn't do anything, which scares you some. He sits there holding a sock, one ankle resting on the other knee. You try to imagine all the things running through his head: *Where are we going to get the money? Will she want to have the baby in the Philippines? When we get back in the fall, will this apartment fit another kid?* These are all things you've asked yourself dozens of times already. You climb onto the bed behind Mark and put your hands on his shoulders, kneading the muscles that are never as tense as they were when he was a farmer, and you whisper into his ear, "We'll pray about it."

And you do, many, many times. You pray as much as you wait. You pray while you're baking cookies, Sarah standing on a chair beside you. You hand her a cup of flour and let her pour it into the bowl and as she does you say, "God bless this cup of flour to make the cookies strong," and Sarah repeats the prayer after you. While you are stirring the thick dough, you give Sarah a few chocolate chips to chew on. She folds her hands and says, "God bless this little snack, Amen." You smile and think, *God bless this little baby inside me, Amen*. Then, as you begin to turn the spoon in the opposite direction, you think, *God bless Sarah, too, Amen*.

On Christmas Eve, Mark drives you and Sarah to your parents' home. He stays until the day after Christmas, and then he has to return to work, but you and Sarah stay until January second. You sleep in your old room and stare at the sanded ceiling like you used to. A circle of light fades out from the center fixture, casting the little sand bumps into sharp relief, the sharpness decreasing toward the edges of the ceiling. You think that you are in the center, in the light fixture, right between the two light bulbs. You have never been without light. You look with some interest and a chilly trepidation at the edges of the ceiling, where scarce light reveals the sand bumps, and you make a promise in your heart that you will stand by your husband to the end of the earth.

When Mark comes back to pick you up, you find out he has asked your parents if you and Sarah could live with them over the summer. Your parents are already making plans for the new baby. They look at you with pride and your mom hugs Sarah and tells her she can ride your old bike with training wheels, the one that has been hanging uselessly from the rafters of their garage since you stopped pedaling it. On the way home to Green Bay, while Sarah is sleeping in her car seat, Mark says, "I've been praying about this. I'm going to miss you, but I think this is best. I think God thinks this is best. Does that make sense?"

And you nod and say you've been praying about it, too. But you don't tell him about the ceiling or your promise. He looks relieved, and you have to admit that you are also relieved. Waiting has become your strong point. You think you'll reach perfection before next fall.

Winter passes quickly, but March and April last forever. You are growing big and your apartment is always too hot. Every time you try to draw in your sketchbook, Sarah demands attention, or the pot of potatoes boils over, or the neighbors turn up their heavy metal music and you hurry to the radio and turn Heaven 101.4 real loud, so eventually you just give up drawing. Mark looks worried whenever he sees you with your eyebrows pinched together and your hands pressed to both sides of your belly. You wonder if he will be glad to leave in May.

When he takes you to your parents' home he cries, but you don't. You tell yourself it's because of the baby. The baby has screwed up your whole system, and when the baby is born, you'll cry, and you'll telephone Mark in the Philippines and cry then, too. You'll be a regular waterfall.

Your birthday is in June, and your mom gives you things for the baby, but she also gives you a Thomas Kinkade calendar. When she bought it on sale she didn't realize it was for the year before, but you don't care. You cut out each picture and use Fun-Tak to hang them on your bedroom wall. When you pray every morning, you do it with your eyes open, looking at one of the pictures, thinking that God lives inside those glowing mansions and cabins and stone houses. What else could make such beautiful light?

The Sunday after your birthday, you are surprised to see a familiar name in the church bulletin. Hank Maxwell— the Reformed Baptist seminarian you used to email and your mom wanted you to marry—is the visiting pastor. You only met him in person once before, but it seems like so long ago, and as you sit in the pew and listen to him introduce himself in that funny lisp that never carried through in his emails and completely shocked you the one time you talked to him in person, you wonder if he even remembers you. Your mom whispers over Sarah's head, "He's still single." You can't believe she says this.

Hank (you don't think of him as Reverend Maxwell) likes to sing. This is something you didn't know about him. Perhaps it is a hobby he acquired since you stopped emailing him. Even with his funny lisp he sings each hymn full into the microphone, savoring each syllable, closing his eyes at the end of each verse. It is quite something to watch, and you are not the only member of the congregation caught up with Hank instead of the hymnbook. He likes to pray, too, you find out as he launches into an impassioned and lengthy praise-petition. You watch him move to his own words, and Sarah nudges you and frowns and blinks her eyes shut several times, indicating that you're supposed to have your eyes closed during prayer. While he preaches, Hank waves his arms and walks so far from the pulpit that the old people in the back pews must not be able to hear him. But you can see he believes what he says. His face gets red and he pulls a handkerchief from his suit pocket to wipe off the sweat. Afterward, you're not sure what he preached about because you were so busy watching him, and, in truth, you were busy thinking about what your life would be like had you married him instead of Mark.

It's easy to avoid Hank after church; people from the congregation flock around him, and you are bombarded by women wanting to know how you're holding up in this hot June weather.

But your dad invites Hank over for dinner.

You try to delay the inevitable by helping your mom in the kitchen, but she is bustling around, perturbed at your dad for inviting someone over without asking if she has enough food in the house. She has enough food, but it's the idea that perturbs her. Your mom shoos you and Sarah out of the kitchen. You try to slink into the sitting room without being noticed, but your large stomach makes slinking impossible. Hank's eyes lock onto yours and you know he recognizes you, but he acts pretty calm, standing to shake your hand and say it's great to see you again, and wow, what a surprise this is that he's eating at your house. You try to explain that this isn't really your house, and that your husband—you emphasize the word *husband*—is on a mission in the Philippines, but this starts your dad on the topic of Mark. Your dad loves to boast about having a son-in-law who is both a dairy farmer and a missionary. You really don't have to talk at all until your mom says dinner is ready, and even during dinner Hank is nice enough not to ask you too many questions. Instead, he strikes up a long and involved conversation with Sarah about learning to ride a bike. Sarah is enamored of Hank, but she is also scared of the bike, even with training wheels. Hank promises to help her ride after dinner, though Mom jumps in and insists he should rest before the evening service. You eat enough food for both you and the baby, drink two glasses of milk, and feel satisfied over this unexpected encounter with an old boyfriend.

You're pretty well exhausted after you help Mom with the dishes, but Hank holds to his promise and helps Sarah with her bike. You tag along, watching from the picnic table.

Sarah understands immediately how to pedal and steer at the same time (a concept you and your parents were unable to get through her head) and Hank doesn't even have to do anything, so he sits by you at the picnic table as Sarah zips between the house and barn.

"This is a pretty farm," he says, looking at the flower garden and the fields of corn and soybeans.

You yawn, overcome by sun and sleep. "It used to look better," you say, staring at the barn that needs shingles and red paint. "When there were cows, it was beautiful." You imagine the barn as Thomas Kinkade would paint it, yellow lights glowing from all the windows.

"Well, what are those?" he asks, pointing to the pasture.

You let out a noise that turns into a snort. "Steer," you say. To explain your contempt, you add, "Nasty, stupid creatures. You just feed them once a day and they eat and sleep in the dirt and get fat. End of story."

"Ah," he says.

You bite back a yawn and ask, "How do you like preaching?"

"Love it. How do you like being married to a missionary?"

You have to force yourself to be alert then, hair-perked-on arms aware that he just asked you a loaded question. You pick through a jumble of words, sorting out a careful answer. "I haven't been for very long. You'll remember, we started out as farmers."

"Ah," he says again, and you wonder what he means by that. He asks, "Do you still paint? Isn't that what you used to do?"

"I draw a little," you say, though you wonder if that's technically a lie, since you haven't drawn in months. *Drew,* you should have said. I *drew* a little.

"What do you draw?" Suddenly he seems terribly interested in your personal life.

You hedge. "Oh, this and that. Pictures of, well, this barn"— you gesture at the barn—"and, you know, myself when I was younger." You pause. "Memories. A lot of memories."

You expect him to say "Ah," but he says, "Oh, I see."

You both watch Sarah successfully dodge a curious barn cat.

You repent. "I haven't really drawn in a while, to tell the truth. I just can't seem to get into it anymore. I figure once the baby is born . . ." You throw up your hands and laugh. Anything can happen once the baby is born. You don't want him to see your little sketches. He wouldn't understand what they mean to you.

"Right, once the baby is born," he says, smiling. Something occurs to him and he says, "You must be very tired. I can watch Sarah if you want to go inside and take a Sunday nap."

You yawn, and that makes both of you laugh. "Maybe I'll take you up on that," you say. "Just tell Sarah to come in whenever you get sleepy yourself."

You stand up and thank him and go inside. But once you're in your room, exhaustion escapes you. You can't even think about sleeping. You sit on your bed and decide to pray, looking at the picture called *Pools of Serenity*. You stare at it so long that at one point you fall asleep with your eyes open. You feel guilty because you haven't actually prayed anything yet, and you don't want to be a past tense *pray-er* the way you've become a past tense *draw-er*, so you close your eyes and force thoughts into your head. You pray for Mark in the Philippines, Sarah, the unborn baby, your parents, Hank. Then suddenly the list unfurls like a roll of golden ribbon. You pray for just about everyone you can think of, and when you're finished, you feel refreshed, as if you've done something better than sleep.

Later, after Anna is born, over a scratchy telephone connection you talk to Mark in the Philippines and tell him how beautiful his daughter is and how much you love him. You and Mark cry together, then laugh when baby Anna starts crying too. You don't remember saying goodbye.

Sarah has come down with the chicken pox and the baby is forbidden to her, which means your mom has to take care of Sarah. You talk to her outside her bedroom door through one of those phones made of string and cardboard tubes. You get her to sing "Onward Christian Soldiers" into her center of an old toilet paper roll, and you are both having fun, you making marching noises on the floor, but then she cries and wants to see you. You cry, too, and in a brave, wavering voice you tell her you are sending your tears through the string, under her door, and if she will hold her cardboard tube to her cheek, they will splash on her like a kiss.

"Is it like a river, Mommy?" she asks in a tiny voice.

"It is a river, darling."

"Peace like a river, Mommy?"

She yawns and you know she is very tired, so you say, "Yes, a river of peace, running right between us," and you hum the song like a lullaby to put her mind to rest. She is quiet, but you keep singing softly, envisioning her sweet, sleeping face, her dark eyelashes, flushed cheeks, wisps of hair fanned out against the pillow. You can see it so clearly that, pulling out your sketchbook and maneuvering it over your baby, you draw the face on paper. Warm with the heat of the newborn, it glows like the paintings in the gallery, if with a shimmer that is felt more than seen.

The Third Painting

It came as a small surprise that my parents left my bedroom untouched. I felt as though I had walked into a time capsule. High school award medals still hung below the shelf of framed postcards from the art museum. Photographs of my old friends were still wedged into the edges of my mirror. I leaned in closer to inspect them. I hadn't seen most of these people since the summer after graduation. A debonair boy in a suit caught my eye. Adam Cok. He and I had been something to each other. We hung out at lunchtime and during after-school activities. We attended the same church and shared many of the same interests. Sometimes, we even said the exact same thing at the same time. Adam and Jenny—two names paired on people's tongues. We had *talent*. We would go far in life.

I had not kept in touch, other than the updates Mom supplied from church gossip. She told me Adam came home after college and landed a graphics art job for a web-design company. Adam no longer attended the same church, but his parents did, and they would undoubtedly be interested in knowing I had returned home.

I wondered whether he had a girlfriend or not. I didn't know if I cared. Maybe.

I sat on my bed, surveying the boxes stacked next to the closet. Some things would need to be unpacked—my clothes, toiletries, art supplies. I glanced at the three paintings wrapped in blankets. I had planned to stash my triptych under the bed, but now I undid the pins and took a fresh look at them. The triptych, three paintings side-by-side, had so completely monopolized my attention that each image was engraved into my brain: the first, an expressionless young woman at a table, eating a solitary meal, her head bowed over the plate. She faced the next section of the triptych—which was the largest canvas and contained the same table in the same kitchen—but on the table rested a beautiful arrangement of cut flowers, two deserted coffee cups, car keys, and a man's hat. The problematic final painting: my initial sketches showed the same young woman shivering alone at night at her kitchen window, the flowers on the table wilting. Alone, cold, all the bright memories behind her. I had tried painting a new third scene, a still life of the flowers, bursting with color and looking like crystals. Permanent until shattered. My professor had volubly praised the new third painting and the weird non-progression of the triptych. I saw it as fake. Fake flowers, a fake life; was the middle painting even true, or was that fake, too? The young woman bought herself the flowers, drank two cups of coffee, set an old hat on the table next to her keys to make the pretense of a friend, excitement, enjoyment. It was something I might do.

I imagined Adam Cok wearing a hat like the one left on the table in the middle painting. It was his sort of hat—retro, jaunty, distinctive. I glanced back at his picture on the mirror, and a poster on the wall behind me caught my attention. *Learn to be content whatever the circumstances.* I sighed. Contentment had never been a strong point. Discontent had sent me home from art school. Discontent kept me from settling down into relationships. Discontent forced me to push my art to its limit. I couldn't give up; I couldn't leave it like that; I couldn't do less than my best. But where did all that bring me to now?

Mom knocked on my door and asked if I would like to help make dinner.

In the kitchen, she peeled potatoes and I chopped carrots. The scrape and chop of busy knives filled the room, but questions hung like a slab of meat between us.

I accidentally cut my fingertip with the knife, and I clutched the bleeding finger with my other hand.

Mom looked at it, concerned. "Is it deep?"

I held it out for inspection. "No, not really."

Mom reached into a cupboard to find the Band-Aids. "Nothing to spoil you on your wedding day."

"Wedding day?" I gave a short laugh.

"It's just an old saying." She peeled the bandage from its wrapper and handed it to me.

"Oh, right." I washed my finger under the faucet, dried it with a paper towel, and tightly applied the bandage. "I thought you knew something I didn't."

Mom returned to the potatoes. "Not at all." Then, hesitatingly, "Is there someone I don't know about?"

"No." I chopped the last of the carrots. "Want these in the pan?"

She shoved the pan closer to me. "You came home suddenly, you know. I thought, maybe there was a reason."

I sighed. "There's a reason, but it might take me awhile to figure it out." And then, "It has to do with art, not men."

"Oh." Mom put the carrots on the stove.

I leaned against the counter. "I think."

On our third date, Adam cooked me dinner at his apartment.

"It has something to do with me, not art," I said, shredding cheese at his counter. I had already explained my triptych to Adam, though I hadn't showed it to him. And I hadn't explained the newest version of the third painting blooming in my mind—one that featured myself: a true self-portrait. It seemed fitting that the expressionless girl in the first painting should completely disappear in the second and come back different in the third, a real person. And how would I portray myself? In love. At least, in hope. Some sort of backlight to produce a radiance around my face.

Outside, the wind picked up and raindrops pelted against Adam's patio door. The weather station had warned of a storm. He looked up from the stir-fry sizzling over his stove. Then he returned his attention to me. "So that's it? Just you? Not anyone else?"

I shrugged. "There was the jilted lover, of course..."

"Ah ha!" Adam pointed at me with his spatula. "I knew it."

I smiled. Already, I had grown to love the easy banter between us. We always knew the right comebacks to each other's jokes. It occurred to me that someday I might be annoyed by this type of familiarity, but, for now, the mutual understanding warmed me. Adam was still mostly the same old Adam of our high school days. I admired his profile, tall and lean before the stove. Whatever had happened to him in the past few years had added intrigue to his character. I liked it.

"No, no jilted lover," I sighed. "No lover at all. No romance, no poetry, no bouquets of flowers delivered to my door. I lived a bare, cold existence." I put down the cheese shredder and looked about the apartment, observing. My gaze fell on one framed photograph of a small bird perched on a stone. In the background an old wall ambled, grew hazy in the distant sky. I recognized this as the Great Wall of China and thought with a twinge of envy how much more interesting Adam's short life had been. "No world traveling for me," I added.

Adam caught my drift and cleared his throat. "That photograph, my dear Jenny," he said with importance, "exemplifies perfectly my own loneliness."

I raised my eyebrows.

Adam nodded. "You see, that small bird, a common thing, but truly beautiful, soon flew away. And what did it leave behind?"

"The Great Wall of China?"

"No, well yes, but no. It left behind a massive, overgrown hulk of the past. Distant, impenetrable. That's all I had."

Rain continued to beat against the windowpanes, and thunder, rumbling distantly before, now cracked as the storm moved in. Adam took the sizzling pan off the stove and divided its contents between two square ceramic plates. It smelled delicious—slightly oily and spiced with ginger.

I stared at the photograph, trying to think of something that could bridge the deep gap between him and that old wall. I wanted to prove that he had no right to be bitter. "Your job?" I asked.

Adam shook his head. "The clients I deal with are stuffy businessmen in suits. They have minds made for numbers, not design. Some days I wonder why I try to please them."

I turned my head, surveying the open apartment some more. "This place? It's your bachelor pad, right? You've done it up nicely."

He pulled some silverware from a drawer. "It's like coming home to myself and finding out just how boring I am." Then, with a bow, he pulled a chair from the table. "Which is why I am delighted to have you here to break up my bachelor blues."

A blinding-white crack caused us both to jump, and a tree branch crashed through Adam's patio door, spraying glass and rain into the apartment, smashing a lamp, sweeping pictures and a mirror from the wall and ripping magazines off the end table. The wind and rain whipped against me, all the fury of the storm now loud and present. A flash of lightning struck nearby, and the lights in the apartment flickered and died. I ducked behind the kitchen counter.

"Are you okay?" Adam yelled over the noise, shielding his face with a bamboo cutting board.

I nodded and yelled back, "What just happened?" Adam handed me his cutting board, which he replaced with the frying pan. It gleamed dully in the storm, strong and metallic like a knight's armor. He led the way to the patio door, hunched against the wind. We picked our way across the living room, a difficult task in the darkness, with no shoes. I felt the prick of glass biting through my thin socks. Flashes of lightning revealed a branch the length of the couch with wet, dark leaves flapping like bats from its subsidiary branches. Adam dropped the frying pan, thrust his arms into the beating leaves, and shoved the whole living thing out the broken patio door. He pulled the cord to the vertical blinds but they fluttered wildly in the wind, hitting him in the face.

He pulled the cord again, turned and shouted, "The bookcase! Help me get the books off."

I was close to the tall bookcase, and I grabbed three books and tossed them toward the kitchen area. Adam came up and swiped almost an entire shelf of books onto the floor, not missing my toes. I bit back a cry and helped him clear the remaining shelves. He pulled and I pushed the heavy oak bookcase toward the broken patio door, grinding glass and twigs into the carpet.

It didn't fit tight against the door, and the wind howled around its edges, but the onslaught had been blocked. I slumped against the bookcase, catching my breath. We heard a whir as the air-conditioning unit started up, and the ceiling lights flicked on again.

Looking around, surveying the damage, I caught my own gaze in the fallen mirror. The expression on my face held neither terror nor excitement, as I would have expected. Instead, I found myself studying myself as an artist studies the bone structure of the face she is drawing —with objection, with careful notes: face has thinned out, hollows in the cheeks, cool gleam in the eyes, warm and cool skin tones round out the jawline, small red gash on the forehead where some glass must have hit. Adam bent down to look at us together in the mirror. Thin, pale face. Shadow of a beard, darker in the cleft of his chin. Rectangular, rimless glasses. Intelligent, dark eyes.

We saw the photograph at the same time.

"Look at the bird," I said, pointing.

"Look at our bird," he said. At least, that's what I thought he said.

The bird, perched on the rock in front of the Great Wall, had fallen to the floor and the glass in front of the photo had cracked in such a way that the spider web network of cracks obliterated the wall but did not cover even one of the bird's feathers.

"You see," I said, "the bird followed you home."

In the days and months to follow, I often thought about that image of myself and Adam and the bird in the mirror. I drew it. I never painted it. I realized, finally, that it did not complete my triptych. Neither did other images that I drew: Adam trying to teach me to dance; the two of us at the table, drinking coffee, Adam reading a magazine, my own nose in a thick, Russian novel; Adam driving his car, hat perched at a jaunty angle on his head, talking merrily as I slouched in the passenger seat, silent and thoughtful.

One fall afternoon, as we drove down a scenic country road, in search of the most beautiful tree, Adam said, "You've been painting."

The road straightened and revealed a farm, gray and run-down but picturesque, with its rickety windmill, pecking chickens, and slanting fence posts.

"How can you tell?" I asked, smiling at the dog dozing outside the barn door.

"You have that look."

"Oh?" I turned my smile to Adam. "And what look is that?"

He slowed the car as we approached another sharp curve. "The look of yellow paint on the side of your nose."

"What?" I covered my nose, and then shouted, "There it is!"

Almost at the same time, Adam braked and pulled to the side. Standing sentinel above a tumbling-down stone wall, which must have marked the border of the farm we had passed, a glowing red maple shivered in the breeze, a bright blanket of leaves beneath it. The tree stood full and strong, a picture of beauty and shelter under the wide, blue sky. Adam slung his camera case around his neck as we got out of the car. We waded carefully through the ditch and the wildflowers growing along the fence line, aware that we were trespassing, but willing to risk it for the sake of finding what we had been searching for.

Under the tree, our complexions rosy from the sun filtering through the brilliant red leaves, I twirled with my arms outstretched. "This must be the most beautiful place in the world!" I said happily.

"Lovely," Adam murmured. He pulled something from his camera case. It wasn't his camera. I stopped twirling, my arms flopping back to my sides, and stared dumbly at him as he kneeled on one knee. He took my hand in one of his, and flipped open a jewelry box with the other. The diamond flashed like fire in its black velvet case.

"Will you marry me, Jenny?" he asked.

I bit my lip and nodded, laughed and tried desperately to wipe the yellow paint from my nose.

Adam smiled. "It's on the other side, but don't you dare touch it. I like it there."

We spent an hour under the red tree, birds twittering in the branches above, insects humming, the fresh, cool breeze rustling the leaves, running across our faces, rippling the long grass. It was an afternoon of sweet nearness and understanding unprecedented in my life. Like two colors swirled together on a palette, our differences combined into a new sensation. I felt more fully charged than ever before, saturated with our love for each other. We drove home, Adam respectfully silent as I admired the new ring on my hand, turning my fingers to see it from different angles. Colors shot out of it, much like the crystalline flowers in the earlier version of the third painting. As I softly touched the spot of paint on my nose, I thought of the wet canvas leaning against the wall of my bedroom at home. It was a picture of a man, facing the center, head bowed over a dinner plate. He sat at the opposite end of the table that the girl in my first painting had occupied alone for so long.

I moved the diamond in the slanting sun streaming through my car window, making a resolution to remove the cryptic middle canvas and replace it with the glass-like bouquet of flowers. Gone were the pretense and mystery. Between the woman and man stood something sparkling and bright, and I prayed it would not be shattered.

A Portrait of Happiness and Love

We drew without him that winter, Maya, Eric and I, and our drawings reflected the emptiness of the room. Dark, shady interiors. Drooping greenery. The new model we hired had a habit of choosing dejected poses, her hands dropping limply at her sides and her body sagging against the props. Maya tried to lighten things up by bringing in upbeat jazz music, but Eric or I would shut it off after a few minutes. The beat jarred our lines, we would say. Eric pulled out his collection of classical music. Mozart, turned really low, suited our mood. Maya never objected. She only pulled her inevitable black sweater closer around her thin body, squinted at the subject and made her elevated announcement, "I'm attempting to draw something worthwhile."

We all tried to draw something worthwhile. Maya's feminist portraits exposed women as unfailingly strong, capable, and collected. Eric sculpted with his pencil, making many light marks until he had constructed something solid. His people rose strong and noble from the scaffolds of his pencil strokes. As for me, I simply enjoyed the drawing. I drew quickly, and I took in as much as possible. Many of my larger works took figure drawing sessions as their subject. I often sat far away from Maya and Eric so I could include them, straddling their drawing horses, their gaze intent on either the model or their paper clipped to the boards in front of them. We all loved drawing, but we missed Patrick.

I had graduated last year, and now I worked on campus as the secretary for the English department, a job I cherished much more than expected. Eric had technically not graduated yet, and he was still working on his final credits, which involved a senior show of his bronze sculptures. Maya had worked in the art department for years, teaching Survey of Art History classes, and presiding over the department's large film-slide library. This semester she had other responsibilities as well, brought her way by Patrick's sabbatical, which he was spending in France, studying Cezanne's mountain. But when it came time for our bi-monthly meeting in the department's drawing studio, we placed our other lives aside. Without the fourth member of our co-op our art suffered, but still we remained faithful, somehow knowing that even from the rural hills of France Patrick would know if we didn't draw.

This is why it came as a surprise, one cold and windy Wednesday evening, to find Patrick's water bottle next to a drawing horse, and Patrick's leather coat draped over the shafts of an easel, and Patrick's favorite prop, a wooden foot stool, placed prominently on the platform. I searched the room for Patrick but only exchanged a startled glance with Eric, who had just arrived and also noticed the same articles of Patrick's presence.

"So he's back," Eric said. "No more moody Mozart masterpieces for us." I knew he respected Patrick, although Eric often failed to express his feelings. "I wish he had given us some warning. I would have brushed up on my human anatomy."

Our usual model arrived: a tall and bony college student named Alexis. When she modeled, she wore the type of swimsuit that professional racing swimmers wear, and she sported two tattoos, one below her left shoulder, the other above her right ankle. Now she shuffled into the room wearing a bathrobe and flip-flops. She climbed onto the platform and switched on the electric heater. Poking the wooden foot stool with an incredulous look, she plopped onto it and asked us, "You want me to sit on this thing, or what?"

I was about to answer, when Patrick entered the room. Actually, he was already at his drawing horse; he had moved in quietly and then cleared his throat to announce his presence.

"You shall pose a number of ways on that stool. The important thing, of course, is not the stool, but your body." He turned his gaze slyly in my direction, obviously pleased at the effect of his entrance. To the model he added, "Please warm yourself while we wait for Professor Mason to join us." His own voice held a great deal of warmth, which softened the sharpness in his words.

He turned his full attention to me, and I was puzzled to find myself blushing. His intelligent eyes studied me, silently summed me up, and then, both to my embarrassment and my relief, turned instead to Eric.

"And how are your heroes and heroines fairing, sir?"

Eric grinned amiably at the older man. "Not slaying any dragons lately. Maybe you can help stir some life into them." He pulled out his drawing from our last session, and the figure, though faithfully sculpted into the page, did indeed look dead.

Patrick raised an eyebrow. "Hmm. You can do better than that, I know. Look there," he pointed a long finger at the girl's hips. "You've forgotten that the pelvis determines the center of gravity." He glanced up a moment at Alexis, who was busy warming her toes at the heater, and I believe he would have made her pose for him had Maya not bustled into the room, balancing her large portfolio, CD player, and a plate of chocolate cookies covered with blue plastic wrap.

"Oh!" she exclaimed, nearly dropping everything. "Oh my. You're back."

Thus began an evening of upsets. Patrick had entirely unsettled our complacent backslide. He upset the model, turning and touching and pointing so much that by the end she looked stiff from fury, a far cry from the droopy, tired Alexis we had formerly drawn. He upset me with that strange and personal look of his, which ignited some fire inside me, a mysterious but potent one which kept my cheeks burning throughout the night. And, most uncharacteristically, Patrick became upset himself.

He had clipped a fresh sheet to his board and moved to my side of the room, a little behind me. As usual, I was drawing quickly, sketching everything in sight—the model, the platform, Eric and Maya, the student drawings pinned to the wall, the plant, the empty drawing horses, the silent CD player, the heater, the spotlight.

"Sandee!" he barked. My pencil jumped, casting a stray line across Maya and the plant.

He drew in a noisy breath, as if to settle himself. I did not turn, but I did meet both Maya's and Eric's eyes, which were equally as startled as mine.

"Sandee," he said again, his voice softer and laced with apology. "Forgive me for causing you to jump." He took another breath and approached my drawing. "Look at this. Is this what you want in your life? Whatever comes, whatever happens to be there?"

I blinked and shook my head no, only because that was expected of me. Only much later, when my life had fewer options, less to choose from, would I contemplate and answer that question truthfully.

"No," he agreed. "You want to find what is interesting. You want to follow your heart. And the same goes for drawing. I didn't come home from France to find my young artist friend drawing boring pictures."

Did he come home because he thought my drawings would be more exciting than what France had to offer? The question made me laugh, and I'm sorry to say I really did chuckle out loud.

"I'm sorry," I said, biting my lower lip. "I think I know what you mean. I shouldn't have laughed."

I looked up at him, and I couldn't fathom what his look meant. It was a reproach, but behind the reproach his expression seemed to manifest doubt. But doubt what? Did he doubt my sincerity? Or maybe my drawing ability? I looked away, and he returned to his drawing horse. He said nothing for the time that remained.

At nine o'clock Maya rose and told us time was up. Alexis hurriedly donned her bathrobe and flip-flops, slapping them indignantly out the door and down the hallway. We watched her go, and then we ate Maya's cookies.

Patrick and Eric left first, and Maya bustled out behind them. As I was about to leave, I noticed a book on Velázquez balanced over the drawing horse nearest the door. I knew Patrick had left it for me, and I picked it up, slowly paging through the color reproductions of his work, enjoying the peopled scenes, the sharp contrasts between dark and light, the emotions beneath the surface. A study of Velázquez would enrich my own art, I knew. It was a challenge of sorts, and I already itched to pick up a pencil. However, I also thought of the book in terms of my relationship with Patrick, which seemed to be blossoming beyond a mere teacher-student dynamic. Subtle hints from the 17th century paintings became a sort of code between the two of us. Here in *Las Meninas* a young princess stood looking directly at me, and in the doorway behind her a man turned, arrested in the moment. Would he continue on his way out the door, or would he come back to the princess? The key was that, for the moment, only those two choices existed. The warm light and use of red in the court portraits seemed to hint at passions that lay beneath the elaborate costumes of the Spanish royalty, and I was sure Patrick meant for me to pick up on passion itself. Enough with the boring depictions of dull drawing sessions! I would dig deeper and display emotions. I would allow myself emotions that I used to think were only for others, not for me. And then, paging through Velázquez's historical and mythological works, I felt Patrick's visual prods even more keenly. Their grandness and importance, coupled with an obvious love of drawing the human body in many dramatic poses, hinted at Patrick's own love for drama and drew out the new feeling between us, a sensation that had indeed become grand and important.

I brought the book home with me. Studied it, read it, dreamed about it. After a full week of imagining myself involved in a mystical art-inspired connection with Patrick, a cold wave of doubt flooded over me as I realized that Patrick's motives in leaving me the book could be nothing more than those of a teacher guiding a student. Perhaps the subtext was the surge of my imagination alone. And then I knew I had let my imagination carry me too far, and I felt such shame that I hid the book in the satchel I took to work, intending to return it to the drawing studio the next day during my lunch break. I banned all blissful thoughts of Patrick and myself poring over Velázquez together, glancing at each other knowingly and shyly as we talked of the artist's merits.

I slipped into the drawing studio the next day, my satchel draped over my shoulder, but I did not drop off the book. I did, however, drop it. As I pulled the book out, he said, from two feet behind me, "Sandee, how nice to run into you." The book thudded to the cement floor, and Patrick, forever light on his feet, sidled around me and snatched it up.

"Ah, and how did you find our friend Velázquez ?" he asked, his eyes warm with interest. He held up the book, so he could view it better. Nervous wreck that I was, I thought he was returning the book to me, and I grabbed at it. After a very brief tug of war, he relinquished it to me and laughed. "You like him very well, I see!"

"Yes, I do," I said, trying hard to laugh naturally, but I did not succeed, and heat poured into my face. "I'm sorry. Here. You may have it. I was . . . I was returning it."

He did not speak as he again took hold of the book. His kind eyes studied me, and then they dropped. In a brisk voice that sounded terribly business-like, he said, "Well, then, I'll see you Wednesday night at our next drawing session."

"Right." I pivoted, ready to beat a path back to my little office near the entrance of the Language Arts building. But he detained me with a hand on my arm.

"Sandee." His voice was very low, and I instinctively moved my head closer to his. A whiff of his cologne, which smelled of open air and oceans, caught me. A small group of students moved toward the drawing studio door we were blocking. His hand still on my arm, he led me further into the room, near the platform which displayed a table of bottles and ceramic bowls. The students who had just entered were chatting and pulling out their still-life drawings, which were obviously based on the display Patrick and I stood next to. Half their attention had turned to us, and I vaguely wondered what they thought of this graying but enigmatic art professor holding the arm of the young secretary they sometimes saw scurrying between the offices of the English professors.

"Sandee, please," he began again, his voice still low. He did not seem to notice our audience. He also did not seem to know how to continue. He let go of my arm and raised the book. Velázquez. He brightened. "Let's discuss this. I know his work can empower your own. How about lunch today?" He looked at me expectantly.

"Um," I glanced at my wrist, which did not have a watch on it, "my lunch is almost over, actually."

It did not faze him in the least. "Then dinner tonight. I'll cook. I love to cook."

I blinked.

"It's settled then!" He beamed at me. "Oh, here, I'll write down my address." He begged a pencil off one of the students, tore a corner from a piece of scrap paper on the floor, scribbled a street name and number, and inserted it as bookmark into Velázquez. Handing it to me, he said, "Seven o'clock. I look forward to it."

I watched him leave, and then opened the book to the marked page. *Las Meninas.* In that moment, I was nothing but embarrassed over having been so tongue-tied, blushing even more over my earlier blush. Later, in my office, as the familiar whir of the copy machine allowed normalcy to calm my nerves, I considered the significance of his page choice. The man caught in indecision in the doorway at the rear had decidedly left. He *was* that man. But (and this question caused me to lose track of the number of copies so I had to start counting over again) was I the princess in the room, or was I perhaps someone else, someone behind the scenes, to whom the man had decided to turn? I both feared and longed for the dinner we would share that night.

As gracious in his home as he was in the classroom, and as accomplished in cooking as in figure drawing, Patrick Stone charmed me. Over an aromatic meal of chicken and angel-hair pasta covered in an herb sauce, he detailed his recent trip to France, highlighting the winter beauties found on the rocky slopes of Paul Cezanne's mountain. The two candles in the center of the table flickered pleasantly in their glass globes, softening his thin, angular face, so animated by the pleasures of telling a good story. Over a thick slice of warm apple pie topped with a brown sugar and cinnamon crumble, he asked me which Velázquez paintings I felt drawn toward. I answered shyly, but not hesitantly, basking in the glow of a good meal, a lovely, warm room, and a man who drew me to himself more than any painting ever created. We moved to his sitting room. Three soft chairs sat among a host of end tables, lamps, rugs, statues, and bookcases. Framed art lined the walls in every available spot. A Tiffany shade covered the nearest lamp, and its soft glow and elegant style warmed the cool doubt inside me. I knew Patrick's interest in me went beyond that of a professor in his student; he looked at me with dark, hopeful eyes, a silent plea for acceptance. The earnestness of his expression caused my own thoughts to turn serious, and I couldn't look away. He pulled his chair closer to the low table directly in front of me and leaned forward. Flustered, I broke eye contact and toyed with the hem of my blouse. He cleared his throat, sat up straight, opened the Velázquez book, acted like the professor. Perhaps my own disappointment showed too transparently, because he softened again and asked, "Would you like to talk about this, or…"

"Yes, let's," I said, and I pointed to the book, opened to a mythological painting showing Apollo in Vulcan's forge.

"Great!" He cleared his throat again, and this time I encouraged him with a shy smile and a nod of the head.

He jumped in. "Well, let's look at this one here. The first thing I notice is the drama. Look at the stunned expression on Vulcan's face. You can't accuse Velázquez of boring us to sleep, right?"

My eyes widened. "Never."

"On one level there are the stark contrasts between dark and light." He looked up to find me staring at him.

"Yes," I said, noticing the gleam of his white teeth, the depth of his deep-set, dark eyes.

"And, uh, look how closely he ties together the subject of the painting, Apollo's announcement that Vulcan's wife has been unfaithful to him, and the dramatic ways he poses the human figures in this realistic blacksmith's forge. It's as if..."

I nodded, reverting my whole attention from the book to his face. "I see."

He smiled, lowered his voice. "As if form and subject could not be separated." He leaned closer, and so did I. Our heads nearly touched above the open book.

"What are you thinking, Sandee?" he asked softly.

I did not know how to say that I was thinking only of him. I blinked, pulled back a little, stammered, "I love it. I mean, it's great—this painting—Velázquez. I want to draw." That last was meant to suggest that studying Velázquez made me want to draw, but Patrick took it to mean I wanted to draw right that minute.

His smile deepened to delight. "Really? So do I. Shall we?"

It was as if he had suggested something illicit, something daring, something in which I was his co-conspirator. I caught his spirit, and I giggled as I nodded. He stood up and motioned for me to follow him. We tiptoed to an adjacent room, which was a small, well-lit studio.

When the bright lights flicked on, the doubt left inside me surfaced. This room wasn't so different from the classroom studios where Patrick instructed. Perhaps the passion he communicated to me over the coffee table had to do with art alone. But I glanced around, and from the unfinished canvases leaning against the walls and the coffee cans filled with brushes, pencils, and mixing knives, I regained some of the intimacy I enjoyed over dinner and during our discussion. This studio had nothing to do with students. I had been invited into the inner sanctuary of his creativity. Now Patrick brought out two large sketchbooks and a can of drawing pencils. He pushed a low stool toward me with his foot, and motioned for me to sit.

"Will this do? I'll draw you, and you draw me. We are our most reliable models, right?" He took a stool a few feet away and immediately began marking his paper, his glances at me very impersonal, but also very thorough. In some small way, I felt violated.

The *habitus* of art kicked in, and I found myself sketching, looking at Patrick not as a person, but as a figure, as part of a composition. No longer did I obsess about the darkness of his eyes; I studied the shape of them, the length of them, the amount of space between them. I knew the space between each eye ought to be the length of one eye, but in Patrick's face, with his eyeballs so deep-set into the caverns of his eye sockets, I found the space to be less than that, and his expression in my sketch was pinched. Was it unattractive? No, in full drawing mode now, I did not think in terms of attraction. His face held character. The jawline, so defined, became a strong diagonal line down which the eye slid toward his torso, where his arms leaned over his own sketchbook. My lines, usually lighter and looser, became controlled and definite. The tension of the moment added weight to my application of graphite to paper. As we drew, time meant little to either of us. Then, I noticed Patrick no longer studying me the way I studied him. Instead of analyzing distances between facial landmarks, he sipped up my image in one long, continuous gaze. His hand lay still against his paper, the pencil slack.

We stared at each other until I had to look down.

"I think we are finished." Glancing at a clock on the wall, he added, "Twenty minutes." He smiled kindly. "In twenty minutes you may have sketched all of the mess I create in my studio. You are so quick."

But his suspicion was not true of this sketch, which contained only a portrait of Patrick from the top of his head to his hands, which I'd caught drawing on the sketchbook. I looked at my work and admitted, "Not this time. This one is different." *You are the reason*, I wanted to say. *You are the only subject I care about now.*

He walked to my side, and he looked. For a long minute, I thought he disapproved. I thought he could read my new-found love for him in the lines of my sketch and he did not know how to respond without breaking my heart. Instead, he said nothing, but quickly brought his drawing of me closer.

Side-by-side, the sketches looked matched. My strong lines complemented his smooth and defined ones, his concentration on the facial features, the rest of my body sketched in. But, mostly, the element that caught us both by surprise was expression. On both faces, we had captured intensity. His gaze unnerved me, though I had drawn it myself. My own gaze in his drawing startled me. Did I really squint like that, shooting out sparks of determination? It seemed so contrary to the way I felt about our new relationship, which was so uncertain, so fluctuating. On his paper, something about me had been decided. Did Patrick decide for me? Did he decide that love would work against the odds, against the difference of age? Or did he only copy that from one flitting phase of my expression?

We looked and looked at the drawings for what seemed like an hour. Finally, I put mine down. I began to apologize for no good reason. "It's completely unlike me— my drawing, I mean. I don't know what came over me."

Patrick put a hand on my shoulder. "Don't, Sandee. Your drawing is good. And so is mine." He pointed at a line on my paper, and seemed about to say something about it, but he stopped himself. "No, I don't need to teach you. We both have accomplished something tonight."

He looked expectantly at me, as if waiting for me to say what it was we had accomplished. I did not know how to say it. Instead, I searched the room for the Velázquez book, finding it on a counter near the door where Patrick had laid it.

Catching my glance, he tightened his grip on my shoulder. "We've talked enough about Velázquez, don't you think?" He took a deep breath. "Tell me, please, what do you think the figure is saying, the figure in your sketch?"

I looked at the pinched expression—pinched in concentration, not pain. I looked at the straight line of his lips, clamped shut. I looked at the shoulders, one raised higher than the other to compensate for the angle at which he was drawing. I said, slowly, "The man is saying, 'This is hard, what I'm doing right now, but it is not too hard.'"

Patrick nodded. "And my figure. What is she saying?"

"She is saying, 'I'll figure it out, if it's the last thing I do.'"

I felt the pressure of his fingertips through my shirt. "Is it really not too hard, Sandee?"

All along I had thought of him as sure of himself. I had thought I was the only one struggling with my emotions. Now I could tell, both in my drawing, and in the slight catch in his voice, he needed reassurance as much as I did. I nodded bravely, and I placed my own fingers on his hand. "We'll figure it out, Patrick."

"But look," he said, pointing again. "He is so old. She is so young and lovely."

"What does it matter," I asked, "if we both look at each other in that way? Your figure and mine—neither of them cares about age. Neither of them cares about loveliness. Just see how they are looking at us!"

He smiled. "They are looking at us as you are looking at me right now."

I blushed and lowered my gaze, but he caught my chin and raised it so I looked at him again.

"I didn't dare think you could care about an old professor like me. But then I drew you, and that woman on my paper wanted desperately to *see* me. Do you understand? Do you understand what that means to someone?" He sighed. "Perhaps it is foolish to think that you are the same as that woman there."

I began to object, but he silenced me.

"But it is not foolishness when I see the same look in your face tonight, wanting to *see* me, not just wanting to hear what I have to say. Am I right?"

Of course he was right. I only had to nod. He gently kissed my forehead. Then he led the way from the bright clarity of his studio to the cramped, comfortable confusion of his sitting room. He once more assumed the role of a gentleman host, gasping at the lateness of the hour, and insisting that he had had a wonderful evening. My heart did not waver. I rejoiced because I knew his kindliness was meant entirely for my sake.

I did not see Patrick until the following Wednesday evening, but I did not expect to see him, and I was not sad. On the contrary, I welcomed the time to mull over our evening together and the love we had dared to uncover. I did not merely think and mull; I prayed. I began a prayer journal, something I had done as a teenager, a habit I had since then fallen out of.

Dear Lord, I wrote, settling against the pillows propped up on my bed. I chewed the end of my pen. How could I begin writing about the impact the past few days had on my heart? For that matter, how could I begin talking intimately to God after a long time of shallow prayers before bed and lukewarm devotion during church services? I decided to stick to the truth. *You know my faults, my pride. I've forgotten You, but You are good enough not to forget me. Forgive me, dear Lord. You brought me Patrick, and I thank You. You brought me love. I thank You. Please continue blessing me. I pray that Patrick may have the same joy I feel right now.*

A picture on the wall caught my attention. It was actually one I painted myself, in high school, when I dreamed of being the type of artist who made a living creating art. Back then, I had no compunctions about copying other paintings. And there it was, my copy of Degas' *The Star (Dancer On Stage)*, which depicts from a high vantage point a ballerina floating gracefully into the spotlight before a carefully jumbled background of painterly strokes and fragments of other dancers waiting their turn on stage. At the time, I admired the painting for the beauty of the white-dressed ballerina, and also because of its different angle and blurred background. Since the time I first framed it, I had that painting hanging where I could see it daily. Now, my senses attuned to a higher, spiritual level, I derived new meaning from it: a picture of what God sees looking at me. The entirety of humanity looms in the background, but I am in clear focus. He will not see only clumsy letters in my prayer journal; He sees truth. He will not solely see me as awkward and uncertain, as I sometimes felt at Patrick's house; He sees a future of love and devotion.

I put down a careful *In Your name, Amen,* set the journal and pen beside my lamp, and sat awake in the dark, dreaming of a marriage with Patrick. I envisioned our life together as graceful and full of beauty. Admiring one another. Admiring art together. I did not envision us talking much. It seemed that our love would transcend words, leaving a quiet, yet richly meaningful marriage which resembles a work of art itself. Before the night was through I had envisioned an idyllic painting of Patrick and I dancing through life, all our imperfections jumbled into the background where they could not encroach upon happiness and love, which we embodied in one beautiful and lasting pose upon center stage.

Had I truly seen our future as God saw it, I would have been afraid. From out of the jumbled background would emerge a certain woman who looked nothing like myself and a man I didn't know yet, but whose piercing expression would puzzle me as I fumbled through my memories for a name or some clue to his disarming familiarity.

Maya and a new model stood next to the heater, discussing poses. The model wore a blanket wrapped around her shoulders, her long dark hair braided down her back. She had large facial features, and even larger glasses. She and Maya smiled big smiles at me when I walked into the studio. Eric, already seated at his drawing horse, nodded in my direction. Patrick's coat hung on an easel, but he was not in the room. My heartbeat ceased for a second at the sight of his coat, brown leather, darkened at the rubbing points. I was nervous because these mutual friends of ours, Maya and Eric, did not know about our dinner together. This evening had the potential to be awkward. How should I act? What would they think if Patrick treated me with the same tenderness of our dinner together? Surely they would notice something, his hand lingering on my back, or the flush of my cheeks. I wished only for grace.

The tension was relieved, but not in any way I would expect. It came through grace, but not mine. From the moment Patrick appeared inside the studio his gaze firmly rested on Kristen, the new model. He looked my way briefly, but I could decipher no hidden messages in that one glance. On the contrary, I sensed that he regarded me coldly, and simultaneously that he regarded Kristen with warmth and excitement. No one could possibly guess that we had shared a romantic evening together. I did not need to worry about *that* anymore.

Patrick had a plan for the evening, and Kristen complied with the grace of an experienced model. He immediately called for thirty-second warm-up poses. Kristen removed the blanket and posed as a runner, a ballerina, a discus-thrower. Her lithe body stretched athletically beneath her red two-piece suit. I sketched with a stick of vine charcoal, its dark lines whipping around my paper while I assured myself that Patrick was just as uncomfortable as I, and it was for that reason that he did not smile my way or look kindly at me.

But he was not uncomfortable. He seemed to be at the height of his comfort. He called for a ten-minute pose. Kristen dropped to her knees, curved her torso out, put both hands on the floor, and looked up at the ceiling.

"Oh yes," he murmured. "Lovely."

We began drawing. I sat at Kristen's side—a profile view. She resembled a model on the beach, shaking out her wet hair, leaning back to receive the sun's kiss. On some other day I would have been entranced, delighted even. It was a superb pose, and probably difficult to hold. I could almost feel the burn in my own neck. However, the confusion and doubt that swam through my head drowned out any finer artistic sensibilities. I drew angrily. I drew unsteadily, my lines layering on top of one another, creating a labored, immature look. I drew only Kristen, and after ten minutes, my drawing looked like something I might have made early in freshman year; it completely lacked meaning and depth.

I hid it beneath my sketchbook before anyone could walk behind and see it.

Patrick approached the stage, smiling gently at Kristen. "How is your neck?" he asked.

Kristen stretched her neck from one direction to another. She grinned and shrugged. "A little sore. Not too bad."

He hesitated, then asked, "Would you be able to do that again for another ten minutes? Maybe later, after the next pose?"

Kristen shrugged again, still smiling. "I think so."

Patrick looked at us. "What do you think? Wasn't that a terrific pose? Could you benefit from more of that one?"

Maya enthusiastically agreed, "Oh yes!"

Eric nodded. "It was a stunner. You're way better than the last model."

We laughed at the memory of sullen Alexis, her flip flops flapping angrily out the door after our last meeting.

Patrick rested his gaze on me. "And you, Sandee?" His voice held nothing beyond the usual. No inflections, no warmth, nothing to tell me that he remembered our evening together. The heater began to hum, and a pencil dropped from Eric's drawing horse to the floor. He leaned down, and when he came back up he stared at me, puzzled and expectant.

I glanced at Kristen, who was looking to me for approval. She was even biting her lower lip.

I nodded, forcing a cheerful tone. "Yes, absolutely! She's a natural, that's for sure."

Patrick turned back to Kristen. "Let's mark your legs then, so you can return to the same place." He dug a roll of masking tape from his portfolio and proceeded to mark around Kristen's legs with bits of tape. I watched him closely, in something of a daze, and I noticed that when he accidentally touched her leg his hand jumped slightly, as if he had touched something hot, or forbidden.

Kristen continued posing, this time in a more relaxed position, and I continued to draw badly. All the time I tried to work out in my head what had happened. I tried to understand what Patrick might be thinking. My faith nose-dived from the spiritual rock it had been perched upon, and my soul rattled like a doomed plane. Under the bright lights that shone upon Kristen, my faith floundered, overcome by jealousy. This was not a confession I would write later, prosaically, in my prayer journal. It curdled inside me, slipped down my right arm, and found release through the HB pencil gripped tightly in my hand. The drawing, terrible as it was, became the evidence that I was guilty.

When Patrick took a stroll behind our drawing horses, he saw my guilt-drawing with all its uncertain lines, scratchy shading, lack of proportion. He did not say anything. He only stood there, watching me draw too fast, working over a portion of Kristen's torso that I had already ruined. He continued to watch, a silent spectator of my downfall. His presence became too much to bear, and I let the pencil drop mid-stroke. I did not turn. He did not speak. But he did move on.

And I forgave him.

When we returned to the beach pose, I attempted only to redeem myself, nothing more. I moved to a new position, a place where the spotlight shone just behind Kristen's upturned head, creating a setting-sun effect. I took my time, something I rarely did. I did not think about Patrick. I did not think about God. I only thought of the woman on my paper, she who emerged slowly from the light behind her. When Maya announced the end of the pose, I had not finished. The others moved around, packing up their materials, stretching. I remained, staring hard at the image I had created. Her facial features lost in the foreshortening of her face, this portrait centered around her long, exposed neck, prominent shoulder blades, taut muscles. She sat on the ground, her legs tucked under her, but every inch of the drawing suggested movement at bay. Her body told us what her face might have belied: this woman had stunning lines, athletic grace, and youthful energy.

Patrick came up behind me. "Sandee," he said, and this time his voice softened so that I knew he was truly thinking about me and not something else. "Sandee, this is a new beginning for you. I'm proud of what you have done."

Eric and Maya, who had been discussing a book they had both read, stopped talking and looked our way. Kristen glanced up from the back of the stage where she was pulling on a pair of sweatpants. Patrick leaned down and kissed my cheek. I could do nothing but smile at him.

Patrick helped me pack up, assisted me into my coat, and we left the room together, his arm around my waist, a goofy smile on my face. We said good-bye loudly, calling it over our shoulders. The others only stared and offered their own weak good-byes.

He led me to his car, a gray Buick. Nothing fancy, but he opened the door for me and bowed deep at the waist. I giggled as I climbed in. When he settled down behind the steering wheel, I asked, "Do you think they have stopped staring yet?"

He smiled in the dark. "I think Eric has whistled one of his long, low whistles, and Maya has put her hands on her hips and said, 'Well!'"

"I'll be hearing from Maya at lunch tomorrow," I said.

Patrick started the car and snapped on the headlights. "And what will you tell her?" he asked, checking over his shoulder as he backed out of the parking stall.

"I will tell her you are madly in love with me!" I said. I did not know where I had gotten the nerve to speak that way, and I fell silent, looking out my window.

He did not respond immediately, but when he did, we were out of the parking lot and on the road heading out of town. "Tell her I am crazy in love. That would be closer to the truth."

"Crazy?" I turned to him. He looked straight ahead, concentrating on his driving. Again, the old finger of doubt touched inside, and I shivered. "What do you mean by that?"

"Last Friday night seems so surreal. I keep thinking it didn't happen the way I remembered it. I keep thinking you are too naïve yet to know your own heart."

The headlights from oncoming traffic bore upon us, and I watched them, transfixed. Inside the car the heater was warming up.

Patrick continued, "I am crazy to think you would be willing to give up the independence you have. You enjoy it, right?"

The words tumbled out of my mouth, "Yes, but, no, love changes that, and I—"

He raised his voice, stopping me from saying more. "You are crazy, too." I heard a smile in his voice. "Your drawing tonight—the last one. It convinced me that you are crazy, too."

The heat pouring from the vent became too much. I fidgeted with the vents, trying to divert the air flow. I also hoped Patrick would keep talking. I did not know what to say anymore. The words he said . . . well, I had never imagined such a conversation. All of my thoughts since last Friday seemed null, as if I had invented a different, a second Patrick, something like a sketch poured from charcoal, as the real one turned out to be someone else. I glanced out the window at the dark trees and the farms lit with yellow yard lights. I wondered vaguely where he was taking me.

Patrick shifted his hands on the steering wheel, and I noticed that he wore leather driving gloves. Disappointingly, they made his hands look like any other man's. I had watched his hands closely many times before, and had grown fond of the deep creases in the joints, the bitten nails, the dexterity of the fingers as they gripped a pencil or brush. His gloved hand came out to touch my face, and I flinched, avoiding it.

"Sandee," he said, returning his hand to the wheel, "last Friday you told me we would find a way to work this out. Maybe I'm getting lazy in my old age . . . I didn't want to try very hard. I came to our co-op tonight convinced that things would go on as before. You and I would be friends, and we would continue our separate lives. I did not want to force anything upon you. You are so young and impressionable, and you have so much promise ahead of you. Why change all that? But then, when I saw your drawing, those new lines that weren't entirely new, but just stronger and better than your old lines—then I knew that you were trying to make it work. You didn't want to stay the same. And you gave me the courage to try as well."

I studied my own hands, ungloved, smudges of charcoal visible even in the dim light. I spread my fingers apart, as if to let his words through. I was hung up on one thought: *He is so different from me*. Before this evening, if asked, I would have recited the many ways Patrick and I were *alike*, even to the point of exaggerating little similarities. Now, his confessions seemed like a foreign language. He was lazy? Never, not industrious Patrick! He didn't want to try? He didn't want to change things? It went against everything he preached in his classes. He thought I was naïve? This hit a nerve. I did not think someone who loved me would call me naïve.

The silence in the car became palpable. I needed to say something. I cleared my throat, but my voice still came out choked. "I prayed for you, Patrick. Since Friday night, I've prayed so much for you and for us."

His own voice held emotion, and it comforted me that he had emotions. It seemed a link that might bridge our differences. "Then your prayers are answered. Am I right?"

"Yes!" I said. "Oh, Patrick . . . "

He took my bare hand in his gloved hand. He squeezed it tightly. "What is it?" he asked huskily.

I watched the yellow center line of the road continue on and on as we drove further and further away from town. Hysteria crept into my voice. "Where are we going, Patrick?"

He was silent for a moment, and then he laughed. I realized that he rarely laughed. Its great, merry sound was unfamiliar yet also attractive. "I'm only driving," he said, at last. "This is something I do often, when I need to think something out. I drive until it's thought out. Then, I turn around and go back home."

"Oh." I stared at the dark scenery flashing past my window. "Are you ready to turn around?" I asked the question shyly; it seemed so personal to ask about his thoughts. It gave me a warm thrill to know I had the right to ask the question, more than anyone else.

He smiled in the dark, patting my hand. "Not quite yet. I have one more thing to think through."

"Oh," I said again. I sat quietly, concentrating on his hand on mine. He did not let go or lessen his grip.

After a minute he said, "I'm thinking about whether a girl would feel offended or maybe rushed if the man she has just learned to love would ask for commitment." He glanced briefly at me. "Maybe you can help me out with this."

I swallowed nervously, but somehow managed to keep the same distant, hypothetical tone he had established. "Being a girl myself," I said, "I would suggest you ask the question, and take the risk on her feelings."

His hand tightened over mine. "Well, then, I think I will. This girl is particularly precious to me, and I am not well-versed in the manners of lovers. It would be pretentious for me to act unsure about my desire to be with her always. Does that make sense to you?"

"I understand. If the girl is anything like myself, she dislikes pretension as much as you."

"Ah." He paused. "Then perhaps you are irritated by this round-about way of asking you to marry me?"

We were approaching a small town, and Patrick slowed down accordingly. I glanced out at the houses, the gas station, the small businesses lining one side of the highway. We stopped at the red light. I did the most impulsive thing I've ever done. Unbuckling my seat belt, I leaned over and kissed Patrick full on the mouth. It was a kiss to surpass any spoken answer. It was a kiss to seal our future. I returned to my seat, breathless, not daring to look at him. The light had changed to green, and Patrick turned on his signal light, drove around the block, and headed back the way we had come.

We sat in silence, suddenly shy with each other. I reached for his hand again.

He glanced my way. "There will be a ring, dearest. We will do the thing properly, later."

I nodded. "Of course."

We both desired a small wedding, and there seemed to be nothing stopping us from getting married soon. We decided on early April, three weeks from our engagement. My father would drive from his home in Chicago to attend the wedding. Patrick's elderly mother chose to stay at her home in Arizona, and his sister would come with her later, in the summer, to visit us. Maya and Eric agreed to be maid-of-honor and best man.

"Everything is coming up roses," I told Maya over lunch at the local sandwich shop.

The news of our engagement had shocked Maya, so much that she had called me three times the evening after I told her the news. She didn't understand how we could have fallen in love without her noticing. Once the idea settled in her brain, however, her enthusiasm had no end.

"Roses, daisies, tulips, chrysanthemums . . . Have you ordered a bouquet yet?"

I shrugged. "No, do I have to do that already?"

Maya glared at me over her sandwich. "Seriously, Sandee. If I weren't here to remind you of things, I think you'd walk into that chapel with your head in a cloud, wearing your pajamas."

I grinned. "That would make an unconventional wedding photo."

"Photos!" Maya's eyes widened. "Please tell me you've hired a photographer."

"Yes. His name is Eric." I stabbed a cucumber in my salad, smiling, waiting for the next exclamation.

"Sandee!"

"We only need a few pictures. He's a good photographer."

Maya groaned and sank back into her chair. "He's your best man. He ought to be *in* the pictures."

"Eric has one of those camera pedestals, and his camera has a delay button. It'll be fine. You worry so much!"

"I worry because you don't!" She took a bite of her sandwich, glaring at me as she chewed.

I laughed. I couldn't stop. Maya wore her ever-present black sweater, and a pair of tinted, thick-rimmed glasses framed her squinting eyes, every bit of her bristling at my inadequacies at planning a wedding. Beneath all that tough exterior, I knew her heart overflowed with gladness and goodwill. Maya was happily married herself, to a philosophy professor at our university—a kind, intelligent man with a full beard and a thoughtful way of pausing before he said anything. I had the strong sense that Maya and her husband sat in bed, deciding which of their unmarried friends they could pair up. She had introduced me to two eligible men on campus previously, but had never even considered Patrick as a possibility.

"I'm sorry," I gasped, my face turning red from laughter. "You are such a dear friend, you know."

Maya bit her lip, hiding a smile. "A dear, stupid friend. I must have been blind. How can two people so obviously meant for each other slip past my radar until they announce their engagement?"

I had regained control over my laughing fit, and I stacked my empty food containers together. "It did happen quickly. You shouldn't be too hard on yourself."

"Quickly isn't the word for it! Patrick comes home unexpectedly from France. He invites you over for dinner. He takes you on a long, strange drive. Boom! You're engaged. Where's the build-up? Where's the getting-to-know-each-other? Where's the fun of letting your best friend invite you two over for dinner?"

"You can still do that," I said.

Maya sipped the last of her water. "Oh, it's not the same." She glanced at me thoughtfully. "Did he happen to tell you why he left France?"

I shrugged, thinking back to his account of France in his warm, candle-lit dining-room. "I think he just had enough."

"Oh."

I could tell she wanted to say something and wasn't sure if she should. I asked, "Did he tell you?"

Maya pulled her black sweater tighter around herself. "He mentioned something about the cold. He said the cold chilled the canvas where his heart paints."

"He said that?"

Maya nodded. "It sounded so tragic and poetic. I hoped you would know what he meant."

Patrick had not mentioned anything like that to me. "I love the way he talks," I said, standing up. "I don't know what it means. It must not be anything too important."

I tried to compose my face, to give the impression that it didn't matter, but the words stayed with me as we returned to campus. *The cold chilled the canvas where his heart paints.* I envisioned blank white canvases and blank, unemotional expressions on the face I had so quickly endeared to my own heart. I would be seeing him in the evening, and I wondered whether I should bring it up.

*

I did not bring it up right away. We saw each other frequently, almost every night. He sometimes met me at the door of the Language Arts building at quitting time. Twice he took me to the campus library where we sat on an old green couch in the basement, studying art books together, perusing the newest art magazines.

We talked about art, but really we were talking about ourselves. He revealed an interest in environmental art. As we studied photographs of fences spanning many hilly miles of country land and lovely circular swirls dug into a beach and filled with frothy water, I noticed that his very being needed space. He couldn't be contained to a studio. The outdoors called him. I began to see that his "thought-provoked drives," as we had dubbed them, were in some ways an art process. He got out, he made a line across the land, and he thought as he went along.

I felt as though he already knew most of my art history, for, as my professor, he had shaped it. Even as we flipped pages in books and magazines, pointing out beautiful things, I allowed him to take the upper hand. I still wanted him to teach me things. I wanted to submit to his authority. Our shoulders touched, our thighs touched, he reached across me to turn pages. We grew less afraid of touching each other. But that was all physical. It took much longer for me to become accustomed to touching his heart, probing it, searching it. He was not a silent, brooding type, but he did have a public face and a private face. I took the small bits of the private Patrick that he offered me. I felt he was generous with that. I tried to be generous with my own private thoughts, and really I poured everything into his hands, in part because I did not have much to begin with.

We came across a picture of ancient Egyptian pottery inlaid with lapis lazuli. One of them depicted an eye. I pointed at the eye. "This is how I envision my inner eye. Bright, open, and there's only one."

He solemnly looked into my two eyes. "The inner eye shines through the outer. Did you know that?"

His gaze was mesmerizing. I shook my head slowly.

He nodded. "Yes, indeed. I think you are right. One of the qualities ancient Egyptians attributed to lapis lazuli was truth and the wisdom to use it. I have watched you. You seek truth with your one, bright eye."

We continued to gaze into each other's eyes. His were dark gray shot with flints of amber. They steadily held mine, and I felt as if I could trust whatever they spoke from inside his deep eye sockets. I whispered, "And the wisdom to use the truth?"

He smiled. "We shall see. Time is young yet."

The next evening he presented me with a beautiful gold ring. Thin, golden branches woven together, surrounding a nest of two lapis lazuli stones and one diamond. We had been in his sitting room, surrounded by all his favorite things. The gilded light shone through the Tiffany lampshade. He pushed the ring across the coffee table, and then caught my hands with both of his. "You see. I have not forgotten," he said. "I only waited for the inspiration, and you provided it yesterday in the library."

My heart pounded because I knew he would ask me again to marry him. And this repetition, of both the question and my answer, seemed an affirmation of God's will for us to marry.

"Will you marry me, forever, as long as we live? Will you be mine in truth and love?"

I loved him more, if possible, for his beautifully-versed proposal. "Yes," I said, and I hid his words in my heart, where they would surface again and again in the years to come, always accompanied with the richness of his soft voice and the intimacy of the warm room we filled with tenderness that night.

And then it did come up—the mysterious poetic line Patrick had given to Maya as an answer to why he had left his sabbatical in France. We had just left Maya's house, a small party she and her husband provided for us before our wedding. Eric had attended with his current girlfriend, a tiny young woman with long golden hair who wore a short pink dress and lacy tights. Fairy-like and ethereal, Eric's antithesis. They pulled away in Eric's pick-up truck as Patrick and I buckled our seatbelts and waved one last time to Maya, who leaned across the doorway.

"She suits him, don't you think?" I asked as I watched Eric's pick-up turn out of sight.

"Opposites attract," he mumbled, shifting into gear.

The party had been full of good cheer and lively conversation. I felt perky and wanted to talk more. "Do you think I'm your opposite?" I smiled at him.

Patrick glanced my way. "No, not quite. I met my opposite. She wasn't much like you."

"Oh." I felt the perkiness drain from me, leaving a void. I asked woodenly, "Where did you meet her?"

"France." He stopped completely at a four-way intersection and looked all ways several times though there was no traffic. "Aix-en-Provence. She worked in a museum."

I remained silent, imagining my dear, familiar Patrick in a foreign country, speaking French to a foreign woman, saying things I wouldn't understand. All at once Patrick's entire history loomed over me like a giant's shadow. I huddled in the car seat, acting cold.

Patrick adjusted the heat controls. "Forgive me, Sandee. It wasn't nice to bring that up." He took a deep breath and exhaled. "I wasn't in love with her, but somehow she got the idea that I was. I may have made a mistake in being too friendly. She took it rather hard when I left."

"Is that why you left early?" I asked, pulled out of my sullenness by curiosity.

"No. I left Aix-en-Provence. I moved to a smaller village, closer to Mt. Sainte-Victoire. My rooms were cold. The food was poor." He shrugged. "My heart wasn't in the right place."

"The cold chilled the canvas where your heart paints," I whispered.

"What?" He jerked his head to look at me, and the steering wheel also jerked. "What did you say?"

I sheepishly repeated myself. "Maya asked me about that. She wanted to know what it meant."

He was silent for two whole blocks. Then I realized we were headed out on a thought-provoked drive again.

"You women," he finally grumbled. "You'll talk about anything."

The road he had chosen was a curvy county route, pitted with potholes from the spring thaws and frosts. We bumped around, the moon shining brightly on the farmland and wooded areas. A flock of big birds near the side of the road startled us, and Patrick hit the brakes.

"Turkeys," he said. The headlights shone on the ungainly birds, which quickly retreated into the field. He resumed driving. "I wonder why they weren't roosting this time of night."

"Do turkeys roost?" I asked vaguely.

"In trees. They can fly, you know. A little ways."

I was thinking about Patrick driving at night, occupied with his thoughts. "Have you ever had an accident on one of your drives?"

He laughed. "If I answer no, I'm sure to hit something around the next bend. If I answer yes, you're going to think I'm not fit to ride with."

"How about the truth?" I asked, trying to make it sound light. It came out sounding defiant and double-edged.

"Well," he said. "A few years ago I totaled my car when I hit a deer." He paused. "And because I think you're not only talking about accidents, I'll add that I left France because of a great unrest in my heart. God was telling me to come home. That is the truth."

I sat silently, mulling over our conversation.

"Any more questions?" he asked, and I recalled many classes in which, after explaining some fine point of artistry to his students, he used the same words to draw us to a conclusion. It was a signal to move on, not a real plea for more questions.

"No."

"Good," he said. "I'm exhausted."

I became alert to his body language, and even in the dark interior of the car, I could see that he was indeed flagging. "Are you?" I asked. "Then why not turn around?"

He glanced my way. "This is your thought-provoked drive, not mine."

I blinked several times. I laughed. "But how would you know . . ."

"When you're finished thinking?" he asked. "I'll know. You're not finished yet." He kept driving forward, his mouth set in a firm line.

I tried to think about what I was thinking about. My mind drew a blank. I giggled again. "I can't even keep a thought in my head."

"It's part of thinking. It's like negative space in a composition. Vital. You'll come through it eventually."

I tried to stop my laughter by staring out the passenger-side window. A dog barked as we passed a farmhouse, and I listened to its howl as we moved away. It was a lonely sound. It made the night seem darker, though I think a cloud slipped over the moon just then. I closed my eyes. An old sensation came upon me, one in which I felt removed from my body. I wondered how it could possibly be me in a car at night with Patrick Stone. How was it possible that *I* had been chosen to be his wife? How was it possible that God had given me this life and not some other, more miserable one? Out of all the people I could have been, why was I me? I felt as if I could choose, right then, to leave the car, escape into the darkness, go back to wherever souls exist before they have been united to a body. I think I even tried it, but the sound of my own breathing pulled me back. I had weight. I had feet cramped uncomfortably under the seat. I moved them out until they stretched under the glove compartment. My eyes opened, and in one sickening moment, the outside world spun unnaturally.

But it was only spinning because Patrick was doing a U-turn in the road. We were on our way home.

The morning of my wedding day I wakened to birds singing. A storm had moved through early the night before, leaving in its wake unseasonably warm temperatures, clear skies, and the delightful smell of damp earth waking up after a long winter. I left my windows open all night. I felt different as I stretched and peered out at the budding trees and bright green grass. I had wondered if being a married woman would change who I was. This morning, I decided on the affirmative. Yes. Even now, being only a few hours from marriage, I had changed. Like the trees, the tulips shooting from the neighbor's garden, the robins pulling up worms, I was entering another season. Out with the old; in with the new.

I surveyed my apartment. I had been packing for the past week, and Patrick had already moved some of my things to his house. The rest would wait until after our short honeymoon, which we would spend in a rustic cabin near a lake only two hours away. Patrick had made all the arrangements, and of all the wedding preparations we had discussed, he had been most excited about our two-night getaway.

I made myself a light breakfast, daydreamed over a glass of orange juice, and smiled at the calendar still hanging from a nail beside my phone. The month of April showcased a Carl Larsson painting entitled "Flowers on the Windowsill." A young girl is carefully and dutifully watering a row of potted plants set on a long windowsill. The window at the end of the row is open. The gentle, vivid watercolor painting warmed me. I imagined the girl reaching the last plant, leaning out the window to watch a bird in its nest, or to sniff the fresh country air. The painting claimed beauty in simplicity. It spoke of lovely details in small moments. It seemed to sum up the goals of my life. I would cheerfully perform my small duties, and then be rewarded with freshness and verve.

I set about my morning humming a tune, and thinking of my upcoming marriage as an open window through which I would gently lean out, accepting all the warm, sun-like qualities I needed to become Sandee Stone, wife.

I had promised to call Maya when I was ready to dress, and I picked up the phone, still humming. I answered her anxious-excited "Hello?" with a sing-song "Good morning, Maya!"

"Are you ready?" she asked.

"I certainly am!" I answered.

"I'll be right over." She hung up.

When she arrived, I complimented her on the efforts she had taken to make herself wedding-proper. A white-silver band accented her short, dark hair. She wore a pink shade of lipstick she must have borrowed from someone else, perhaps Eric's new girlfriend. Her dress was a long, flowing pastel green, sleeveless and topped with a short black sweater-jacket. A silver necklace with a large pink stone completed her look of Maya-in-the-spring.

"You are still in blue jeans!" she exclaimed, horrified.

"But Maya, I called you over so you could help me dress. That was the plan."

She threw up her hands. "I thought I'd straighten out your wrinkles, finish zipping your zipper. The wedding is at ten!"

"And it is only eight-thirty. Plenty of time. My dress is hanging up in the bedroom."

Maya buzzed about me, getting me ready. When she ransacked the bathroom and the boxes I had already packed, looking for hairspray, I stopped in front of the mirror. Behind me, the curtains flapped in the breeze, and my cheeks were flushed from the excitement and the new spring air. The effect was enchanting, and I wrapped a stray tendril of my brown hair behind an ear. I could barely believe this was me. I had no need of a fancy dress, so, with Maya's help, I had chosen a knee-length white one trimmed in lace. It had cap sleeves, a fitted waist, and it looked just right with the short, filmy veil attached to the tiara in my hair. Normally, I had a calm, pale, studious look, but this morning I saw more love shining through my expression, brightening my face. Did this happen to every woman on her wedding day? My thoughts so occupied with Patrick, I could only say that what I felt had its origin in him. Other women, with their other husbands —I couldn't even imagine how they felt. All the other scenarios I could recall seemed too strange and different from my case. I believed God ordained marriage from the beginning of time, but it seemed that God had taken particular care with mine. How else could this spectacular thing be happening to me? To what other than God's hand could I attribute the rapid and perfect turn of events since Patrick's return from France? I concluded that there must be something important, some milestone in the history of our lives that would matter a great deal in the scheme of God's plans. Perhaps a child or grandchild of ours would be a renowned Christian. Perhaps some future artwork, either Patrick's or mine, would help bring about a more beautiful aesthetic. I shook my head, trying to clear it. There were things God never meant for us to know.

Maya rushed in, triumphantly holding a can of hairspray. She stopped behind me, looking at my image in the mirror. Her mouth was open, ready to speak. She closed it and stared, the hand holding the hairspray dropping to her side. When she did speak, her voice sounded close to tears.

"Sandee, girl, this is it. You're going to be Mrs. Patrick Stone, and all of a sudden, I can't think of anything more wrong for you."

I stared at her in the mirror. "Excuse me?"

She heaved a sigh. "I don't know. You look so lovely, so young, so *everlasting*. When you marry Patrick, your life is going to close in on you. You'll be finite."

"This is not a good pep talk, Maya."

"Oh, I don't have an ounce of tact in me. I just see you dressed in white, standing so firm on those strappy little heels, and I want to snap a photo so I can paint a picture of you this way, later."

"When I'm old and married and of no use to anyone?"

"When you're old and married and only useful to Patrick. The greedy, old thing." She wielded her can and sprayed a cloud around my ear, where the strand of hair wouldn't stay in the right place.

"You can do that, you know. There will be pictures." I stood still, trying not to sneeze.

"Oh, I just don't want you to get married. I'm like that. Ignore me."

I said nothing. She fussed with my hair.

She added, "I was even like that at my own wedding. I nearly didn't walk down the aisle."

"You see, Maya. You are useful to me, and you are married."

"Yes, but Alan is not Patrick. Alan is what they call an abdicator."

"Abdicator?" It sounded criminal, and I couldn't imagine Maya's thoughtful, gentle husband doing any type of crime.

"He abdicates his headship duties to me." She pulled at my veil to make sure it was firmly attached. "We took a marriage class at our church once. That's what I learned."

This was getting to be too much for me, and one of my laughing fits interrupted our debate.

Maya put her hands on her hips and ordered me to turn around. I did, but I was bent over laughing. She wagged a finger at me.

"Now you stop right now, young lady. Don't you dare get all blotched in the face because you were laughing at me! Patrick won't be an abdicator, and that's a good thing for you. He'll give you guidelines to live by, and you are probably just the sort who appreciates guidelines. Right?"

I nodded, gasping for breath. The laughing stopped, and I took a deep breath. "Right. I love being ordered around." It occurred to me that I really *did* like being ordered around, by Patrick. Even when he was my teacher, I liked it most when he told me in no uncertain words what I had done wrong and what I needed to do to fix the error. This seemed like another thread in the beautiful weaving of our predestined marriage, which I could hardly wait to begin living.

I cheered up, my laughing fit forgotten. "You're right, Maya, about almost everything." I smiled, not insincerely, in her direction.

✳

We chose to be married in the university chapel, a sloping room with tall stained-glass windows on two sides, and short benches padded with dark red cushions. This chapel dated back to the time when the university had been affiliated with a Lutheran church, but now it served as a place for students to pray, meditate, and hold small Bible studies. Here I had attended evening recitals, wherein my musical friends performed by the chromatic light of the tiered chandelier that hung from the ceiling.

In mid-morning, with bright sunlight pouring through the colored panes like heaven's own glow filtered through the reds, blues and golds, I felt an intimate connection with each person inside the chapel. My father, pale and solemn-looking in a gray suit and blue tie, sat in the front bench beside Alan, whose beard could not hide his kind smile. On the other side of the aisle sat Karina, Eric's girlfriend, small and fairy-like in a yellow sleeveless dress, her face lucent with glittery makeup. Maya stood behind me, holding my small bouquet of yellow and white roses. I could feel her stillness and her nearness, and this was a comfort. Eric stood very straight behind Patrick, his blond hair slicked down, his hands clasped in front. He wore a smart-looking vest and dress pants, and the yellow rose pinned to the vest gave him the smooth look of a dandy. The minister, who usually stood official and stately behind the high pulpit in front of my church, now seemed friendly and familiar as he held his white leather Bible close to the space between myself and Patrick. Patrick, dear Patrick, held both my hands in his large ones. Hands I loved, deeply grooved at the joints, bony and firm. Though he was not a large man, his presence filled mine, as though only then was I made aware of an absence that had existed inside of me, and I felt that this great awareness of each other was what the minister meant when he said we would become one. Every rise of his chest, every small turn of his head, each time he squeezed my fingers, I could feel as if I had done it myself. I did not merely *notice* Patrick; I sensed why Patrick moved, why he breathed, why he caught my eye and nodded encouragingly. In all this closeness of bodies and sentiments, I could not detach my own mind enough to follow the ceremony. It was performed outside of us, the voice of the minister a clear, rolling music inside me, even as the intent of the words did not register. It was for this reason that I was surprised when Patrick pulled me close and kissed me, beamed down at me, and then turned me around so we could be congratulated by the others.

The hugs, the wide, happy smiles, the general noise of six voices speaking at once blew away the intimacy and taste of holiness I had experienced moments ago. It did not do away my love or the conviction that I had just done the most important thing in my life. I did, however, feel strange that I was not immediately whisked away to be alone with Patrick, and instead had to share my new husband before I even had the chance to hold him.

As planned, we left the chapel and drove to Leo's, the fanciest restaurant in town. My father rode with Patrick and I, in the backseat of Patrick's car, and I made small-talk with him as we drove, feeling guilty and strange for not knowing how to include Patrick in the conversation. Thankfully, he did not seem bothered by this, and his warm gaze fell on me several times when he should have been watching the road.

Glancing between Patrick and my father, I noticed they did not look much different in age. Patrick's face had the chiseled, rugged look of someone who has weathered life, and gray hairs peppered his goatee, making him look older than thirty-nine. My father, on the other hand, had a thick, full head of graying hair and a smooth, placid face which belied his years. I did not feel like the bride of a much older man, but seeing the two of them together did make me wonder if they thought of me as young and inexperienced—an innocent.

Patrick dropped us off at the door, and then drove off to park the car. Dad and I walked into the restaurant waiting area. He had arrived the day before, and Patrick and I had spent the evening with him, but this was the first time I was alone with my father. We sat on a bench by the coat hangers, and I asked shyly, "So what do you think, Dad?"

He shrugged a little and laughed. "About Patrick? Good man. Easy to talk to."

My father was an accountant in Chicago. He had always been reliable and trustworthy, but he was not a social man. He kept his thoughts well-hid, and he didn't seem to know how to retrieve them from their hiding spots. A man who could draw words out of him was a worthy man. I felt proud of Patrick for having this gift.

"Did you think I ever might marry someone like him?" I asked.

"Well, I don't think I had a particular type of man in mind, Sandee. I am . . . surprised . . . that it all happened so quickly. You know your mother and I dated for two years before our engagement."

I was surprised that he mentioned Mother. Since her death six years ago, he seldom mentioned her. She died of a painful cancer, and when she was gone, a massive void opened between Dad and I. He was grateful, I think, that I left the state to attend college. Dad could survive loneliness better when he was truly alone.

I nodded. "I know. It happened so differently from anything I imagined."

Patrick found us just then, and the others were with him. Dad and I stood up, and the hostess led us to our reserved table.

We dined on steak and salads, garlic mashed potatoes and corn, and dainty cups of rice pudding sprinkled with nutmeg. I smiled pleasantly, kept up and contributed to the conversation, ate heartily, the entire time impatiently awaiting the end of it all. This dinner seemed excessive. I did not know then that married life sometimes worked best in the company of others. I thought being married to Patrick primarily meant having him to myself. I enjoyed the funny way Eric passed Maya the basket of rolls over and over, knowing full well that Maya was always on a diet and would only eat half a roll. The other half went to her husband, who was never on a diet, and sweetly accepted whatever Maya thought was too much for herself. I even enjoyed the story Patrick told about a naïve tourist in France who approached Patrick, asking him if he knew where Paul Cezanne lived and if he accepted visitors. I glanced at my father, not sure if he understood the joke, but he was laughing and apparently enjoying himself. He did not say much, but, again, he usually didn't. The fairy-like Karina settled in closer and closer to Eric. When the waitress arrived with dessert, Eric had his arm around her shoulders, and her head nestled close to his. She quietly watched us, and I knew how she felt. She had wearied of being social, and she wanted to leave with Eric and find some peace. I, too, longed for that peace. Though Patrick sat right next to me, and though he paid thoughtful attention to me during the dinner, the presence of the others, and the presence of everyone eating inside the restaurant, distracted me. I could no longer sense his thoughts, his motives. I did not feel that holy oneness I had felt during the ceremony. I only felt like a lonely, uncertain new bride lost in an atmosphere of celebration and merriment.

I began to examine the artwork on the restaurant walls. Even that failed to perk me up. Framed black and white photographs of local landmarks (the deer and fawn statue by the country club, the gurgling brook and footbridge, the old mill) hung below a running border of stenciled pineapples. The two did not complement each other, and I found myself suddenly disliking Leo's Restaurant.

I noticed more unfavorable things by the time Patrick finally made his move to leave. As he scraped his chair away from the table, my father quietly insisted that he would pay the entire bill. Eric and Karina slipped out with barely a salute in our direction. Maya rushed over to hug me one last time, and Alan shook my hand again. They left, Maya calling over her shoulder that I ought to pack extra blankets for the cabin, just in case. Patrick and I waited for Dad, and he held my hand and squeezed it. In a whisper, he asked, "Did you see the pineapples?"

A rush of warmth and relief spread over me, and I caught myself just before I slipped into a laughing fit. Instead I glowered and whispered, "They were almost as bad as the fake carnations in the plastic bud vases."

As the three of us exited the restaurant, the warm spring air took me into its embrace and I wanted to skip like a little girl. I did a little two-step instead. Dad and Patrick both looked at me strangely, and I giggled.

"I'm just happy, that's all," I said. And that was the truth. Above all, I was happy. Happy to be alive, happy to be at Patrick's side for the rest of our life together, happy to be in Leo's Restaurant parking lot with solid ground under my sandals and the clean spring breeze blowing through my hair like a promise sent from the lapis lazuli sky above.

The drive to our rented cabin on the lake took longer than we expected. Patrick could not seem to find the right roads, and he wouldn't let me open the map. "We'll get there," he said. "Don't worry. It will show up." It didn't seem to be a question of male pride at stake. He simply enjoyed the meandering drive through the wooded countryside.

"Is this a thought-provoked drive?" I asked.

He shrugged. "I'm thinking about you. Does that count?"

It did count, and I blushed, though I didn't want him to notice.

"Your ears are bright red."

I laughed out my window at the stampede of tree trunks. "It's this whole getting married thing," I explained. "It's making me . . ." I searched for the right word.

"Embarrassed? Frightened? Unsure of yourself?"

"Giddy."

He snorted. "Giddy. Right." He glanced sideways at me. "Not embarrassed, frightened, or unsure of yourself?"

I glanced sideways at him and quickly shook my head. "Nope." I paused. "Should I be?"

"Some people would be embarrassed to be with me. Maybe even frightened. Who knows where I might take them? I don't even know where I am."

"Sounds like an adventure," I said. "I love adventures." This was true. Although my natural timidity sometimes impeded me, I did crave new things, which was partly what gave me the desire to major in art. Art had unclear boundaries, and it had built-in structure. Some things in art, like figure drawing, put me in places I had never been before. Other things, like Patrick's color studies, appealed to the practical part of me that liked systems and order. Applying this to my very recent marriage, I thought of Patrick as both a practical choice and a mystery who would make life intriguing.

The adventure of finding our honeymoon destination without a map ended when we stumbled upon a town and decided to buy a bite to eat at the local sandwich shop. The owner, a white-haired man with sharp eyes and a dignified nod of the head, sat across the counter from us as we ate. We were his only customers.

"You passing through?" he asked, leaning back in his stool, arms crossed over his thick middle.

Patrick nodded.

"Mind if I ask where you're headed?"

"Round Lake," Patrick said.

The owner nodded knowingly. "Nice place."

"We're on our honeymoon," I said, smiling at Patrick.

"Is that right?" He whistled under his breath, thought a moment. "Well, a cabin on the lake is just right for two love birds. My own wife, she wanted a cruise. Busiest, noisiest trip we ever took. She loved every minute of it, but I thought I'd made some sort of mistake marrying her. I was sick in bed half the time, and when I could get up and walk around, I had a headache from all the racket going on. Now, I like a good conversation here at the shop, but when I'm on vacation, I want to rest my ears, if you know what I mean."

He gave us another sharp look. "Yes sir, you've caught yourself a pretty-looking spring chick. I congratulate you both."

I laughed at being called a spring chick. I wondered if people would give me such compliments twenty years down the road, if the differences in our age would still be so obvious, and imagined myself using Patrick's age as an excuse to feel young and spry.

"Thank you," Patrick said, glancing slyly at me. "She was my student once. I think I've chosen the top of the class."

The owner chuckled. "Is that right? I don't hear stories like that too often. What subject do you teach?"

"Art." Patrick bit a large chunk of his sandwich.

He slapped his knee. "Well now, if that doesn't remind me of this artist fellow who stopped in, wanting to know all the scenic spots in the area. I told him this was God's country, and he could look in any direction to find a pretty picture. Then another customer recommended Round Lake, which is where you're headed. 'Go north on County V until you reach Sunset Drive. Take a left,' he said, 'and you'll run into the sweetest bit of paradise in these parts.' I remember it well because that artist fellow acted so grateful to the other customer, and I always wondered if he painted a picture of the lake."

I watched Patrick's expression as the owner gave out the directions to our honeymoon destination. Patrick said nothing, but his shoulders slumped slightly. We finished our food, thanked the owner, and climbed back into the car. As Patrick pulled onto County V, going north, he shrugged and said, "At least we gave the old guy a new story to spread around town."

"It might have been dark before we found the place on our own," I added.

"Would that be so bad?"

I smiled. "Not when I'm in the car with you."

He patted my hand gently. "Good answer."

The owner of the sandwich shop had not exaggerated. Our cabin, nestled between some very tall pine trees and overlooking a gently-rippled lake, held all the charm and romanticism of a Terry Redlin landscape painting. I had a love-hate relationship with Redlin's art. In my pre-college years, I loved him. Copied his paintings. Bought a coffee mug with my favorite Redlin winter scene printed on the side. I cut a small painting called "Sundown" from a magazine. Geese fly over a farm huddled within the cold fall landscape. I taped it inside my high school locker door. During my mother's illness, I imagined myself tucked away in that farm, safe from the onslaught of disease and worry that ruined her. Only there, inside my imagined refuge, could I dare to dream of what my own future might be like, taking wing with the birds that flew so freely and determinedly away from the harsh elements. However, during college, I learned to hate Redlin's mass-produced, market-driven sentimentality. I hid the coffee mug in a box of old sweaters so none of my new college friends would find it. It's not that I hated all the money he made off his art; I hated his ability to produce exactly what the public wanted to buy. My impassioned professors' lectures, especially those that touted art for art's sake, fell highhandedly on Redlin's work. Shouldn't good art take things beyond the limits of the average consumer? Shouldn't Terry Redlin grow, go beyond his picturesque farm scenes and reminiscent Americana themes? Wasn't he taking advantage of the circumstances for his own profit? Most of the time, I answered these questions with a resounding "Yes!" Tonight, standing in front of the rugged lakeside cabin, the sun beginning to stain the sky pink and purple, trees darkening into a deepness that bespoke ages past, all thoughts of Redlin reached beyond the narrow questions of marketability and aesthetics. He was, or rather his paintings were, works of genius that resonated with remarkable moments of real life, such as my first night married to Patrick Stone.

His dreams and mine concerning perfect honeymoons fell pleasantly along the same lines: romance, adventure, engaging conversation, deep and meaningful silence. We lived like hero and heroine at the end of a happy story. On one of our walks, this one taking us along a wooded side of the lake, he asked, "Have you thought much about the *wisdom* of being married?"

Though the question popped out of a long silence in which I had been admiring the slants of light that shone through the treetops, I did not consider it strange. I pondered it for a minute. "Do you mean the wisdom of being married to you? Or the wisdom of anyone being married?"

"You," he said. "Was it wise for you to marry me?"

"I don't know." I thought a bit, and added in a sly voice, "It certainly was wise for *you* to marry *me*."

To my jest, Patrick nodded, indicating a wholehearted agreement. "Yes, no doubt it was! Here I am, getting older, beginning to wonder if I might be bored with my career, and needing inspiration to keep my spirit alive. There you are, young and full of life and spirit, enough to fuel both of us for quite some time." Here we paused at an overlook of the lake, which lapped the bottom of the cliff we stood upon, about fifteen feet below. Sea gulls swooped low over the dark, blue-green surface, as if diving for jewels in the bright, sparkling water. Patrick took my hand, and I squinted at his face. A wistful, serious expression puzzled me, an expression I was to remember later in our marriage, when it would recur more regularly. He said, "But I'm afraid, when your spirit begins to ebb, then mine won't be enough for you."

That this would ever be true seemed absurd to me then, and I quickly protested, but he only smiled, and his gaze reached beyond my own and touched something older than me. I shivered, and he put his hand on my back, gently leading me up the wooded trail.

That evening, as we silently contemplated the next morning's return home, the sun began to set and the suddenly cool air woke me from my musings. I rose from the stair we had been sitting on, as did Patrick. We walked hand-in-hand to the lake shore and stepped carefully along a string of large, gray rocks. We arranged ourselves in such a way that, sitting, we could rest our feet on a small rock. The water lapped gently beneath our legs, and the stone we sat on felt cold and unyielding. I could not take my eyes off the sky and water as they transformed from bright and sparkling to dark and mysterious. These transformations subdued my mind's drama, and the subtleties of colors changing before my eyes transfixed me.

"What are you thinking about?" Patrick asked, quietly, his voice cutting into my reverie.

"Oh, I was thinking of colors. I wish I had brought some paints along." I did suddenly long for a canvas and paintbrush. My fingers ached to be busy. I folded them tightly in my lap.

"Mmm." He nodded. "I know what you mean. I can see myself mixing that peachy-red color, and the smoky gray-green in the water could be repeated in that cloud drifting above the sun."

"We'd never get it in time," I said. "It's changing too quickly."

Patrick grunted. "Makes you respect the plein-air artists a little more."

I had tried painting outdoors two or three times in my life, but the practice didn't stick with me. "How did they do it?"

He shrugged. "Persistence, memory, high observation skills. In many cases, they tried to come back the next day at the same time to regain at least some of the original atmosphere."

"Nothing that could be captured in a photograph," I added, rubbing my arms where goose bumps had risen.

"If it could be captured in a photograph, why paint a picture?"

"Is that why you paint?" I asked, feeling the conversation had drawn deeper than it had begun. "To *capture* what you see?"

He looked at me, and I stared at him, at last really seeing his weathered face, the graying goatee, the inset eyes shadowed by prominent brows. His thin lips, lacking much color, seemed set to say something, but hesitated. *This was the man I married*, I realized, and the thought frightened me because he seemed so complete within himself. I did not see myself needed.

He spoke, "I paint and draw and create art to capture something. I'm not always sure what the something is. And then I release it to whomever wants to look into my work."

"Oh," I said, pulling my knees up and wrapping my arms around them. I turned as the sun dropped behind the tree line, leaving an orange smear in the sky. Gray shadow formed like a cloud around and between us, and the sound of water working away at the shore and the frogs creaking escalated to such a pitch that I was shocked when the sound of Patrick's voice sounded clearly above them.

"It was good of you to make me talk about my art, Sandee. Anyone else, and I would have rattled off some inane answer just to satisfy them." He put his warm hand on my arm. "Come, let's go back."

But something was holding me there on the cold rock, in the deepening dark, with the night gathering its forces around me. I wanted him to pull me back to the cabin and the warmth of our togetherness. I did not want to go willingly. So I said, "One more question, please."

He did not remove his hand from my arm. "Okay."

I cleared my throat. "It's about God. Why have we not talked about Him?"

"We have," he began.

"No, not really."

Silence. I imagined the hesitant line of his lips, but all I could really see was a dark shape of Patrick, with darker shadows suggesting features and body parts.

"Then it's because I don't know what to say about God."

"Is He great, to you? Is He majestic?"

"Great? Yes, but not to me. He is great without me. He is majestic without me. Within me, He is mystery."

"But He is within you, Patrick?"

"Yes." He tapped his chest, over his heart. "He lives here. I know that."

I felt that he thought the conversation over, so just before I allowed him to bring me to my feet, I asked, "One more thing?"

"Of course."

"Could you paint it? That knowledge that He is in your heart, that you are one of His?"

He hesitated again, struggling for a truthful response. Finally, he said, "No. I haven't captured God or my own faith in Him. Faith is a gift, and I can't release it unless He lets me."

I nodded, strangely satisfied that some spiritual hierarchy had been established in the darkness, at the edge of abyss, at the beginning of this new period of life. We slowly picked our way off the rocks, using the LED light from Patrick's cell phone as a guide. In the cabin we did not continue our serious discussions, but our playful exchanges were accompanied by shy smiles and soft touches. Before we slept, he whispered, "Only you, Sandee. Only you could make me feel as if I was a student again, stumbling over the answers."

*

His house. No, our house. I knew I had to get used to it, but the house we now shared as husband and wife had Patrick's personality written all over it. The walls could barely be seen, so I had never noticed that the kitchen was painted a light rose color. My second morning living there, as I opened the refrigerator door to see if Patrick bought any orange juice, I discovered the paint color. Removing a poster that announced an art show from ten years back, I examined the walls carefully and decided I liked them. Feminine, soft, petal-like. I read the poster at arm's length. It featured a man who made collages from found objects such as wire, bottle caps, twine, and pieces of laminate flooring.

Patrick walked in. I looked up from the poster and said, "A little strange, don't you think?"

His eyebrows shot up. "Strange, indeed. The fellow put a few old things together and out came a new order, a universe of objects arranged according to his design, a really impressive body of work. The poster doesn't do it justice."

"Oh." I stuck the poster back on the wall. "I just noticed the lovely walls."

"Lovely?"

"The color, Patrick."

"Pink."

I put my hands on my hips. "And you call yourself an artist."

"I avoid pink in my art." He took down two glasses from the cupboard. "The walls came that way when I bought the house."

"Well, I think they are lovely. Wouldn't it be nice if we saw more of them?" I said this in the least offensive way possible. I loved Patrick and did not want to do anything to irk him. If he had decided to find more posters of obscure art shows for the sheer purpose of pasting them to cover the remaining wall space, I would not have minded.

In those early days of our marriage, everything he said was charmed, and he must have thought the same thing about me because he stroked my tousled, out-of-bed hair and said, "Do what you like to the house, my dear. If you like the walls, then uncover them!"

He kissed me and poured a large glass of orange juice for the both of us. I found some bowls, spoons, and a box of cereal. We ate at the stools next to the counter, and I plotted what I would do to uncover the pretty, rose-colored walls. Then, because I noticed Patrick ruminating over the art show poster, I decided I wouldn't do anything just yet. I would get used to the house first.

Every time our house entered my thoughts it came as "the house," and I began referring to it in this way.

After a month of living in the house, I began to make some changes, tentatively at first, to test Patrick's response. I took down a few of his things and made a neat pile of them on his studio counter. My own things, which largely remained in moving boxes in a row along the bedroom wall, began to come out and work their way into the network of Patrick's belongings. I replaced his calendar of scenic America with my own artsy one. The month of May featured a lovely painting called "Time For Tea" by Robert Walker Macbeth. This unpeopled scene invited the viewer into a delightfully decorated porch which held a small table set for tea. I gazed at the painting, loving its intimacy and the casual way the surroundings suggested a harmonious relationship. The house I lived in contrasted sharply with this scene, seemed foreign and cold. To be fair, I did enjoy the sitting room with its Tiffany lamp and crowded appeal, but, even so, I did not envision myself curling up in a chair with a good book and a glass of iced tea. I knew it as a place to sit with Patrick and discuss the day's events. My "alone time," which at first I did not want, but which Patrick insisted upon, usually came after dinner. Patrick retreated to his studio and I headed outdoors to mow the small lawn or pull weeds from the flower bed and around the house.

Classes ended for the year and we both had more time on our hands. Patrick could spend hours in his studio, to the point that it seemed he sacrificed much of his studio time so he could do things with me. We took long drives. We bought bicycles and tried them out on the local trail, deciding in the end that we preferred walking because we had to stop cycling each time we wanted to say something. We attended an opera with Maya and Alan. Patrick's good taste in anything that had to do with the beautiful impressed me, and I easily slipped into the role of a newcomer to the Fine Arts, the *naïve one*, introduced by a connoisseur to all they had to offer. This role was a little different than that of a student being taught by a professor. Instead of challenging me, Patrick pampered me. When we went to a museum together, or when he showed me a book on a new artist, his delight in sharing these things with me shone through his tender look, rung clearly through every word he spoke. Once, he wrapped an attractive edition of Degas' ballerina paintings in pretty pink paper. He left it on the kitchen counter with a note: *These paintings are feminine and full of life, just like you, my dear. Love, Patrick.*

Then, Patrick's mother and sister visited us for a week. They arrived in a rental. Patrick's sister, a short, stocky woman in her forties who wore khaki pants and a navy polo shirt, assisted her mother from the passenger side. The old woman had a cane, short, curly, dyed-auburn hair, and she wore a denim dress trimmed in lace. "We've already been to the motel," she announced as soon as she spied me. The sister, Gracie, shut the car door and led her mother up the walk, holding her arm. "It's a convenient room, and it will do, but it is quite boring. I will have to sleep under gray covers and walk on a gray carpet and stare at white wallpaper striped with gray. Hopefully Patrick's house is more exciting. I would go bonkers living in a place like that."

I invited them in, explaining that Patrick wasn't there at the moment. She demanded a tour of the house, and, after poking her nose into each room and tapping each floor with her cane to test its strength, she said, "Acceptable. But he could have done better. How do you *breathe* in here, my dear? It's so cramped and stuffy. Gracie, would you open the window behind that wooden totem-pole-sculpture thing?"

Gracie silently and swiftly moved the totem-pole-sculpture thing and opened the window, which squeaked from lack of use. Her mother poked the green armchair with her cane, coughed over some pretended dust, and finally settled into it. She sighed and closed her eyes for a moment. Upon opening them, she found me staring. "Well then," she said, "you may call me Mother. I understand yours is no longer with us. I won't try to be a substitute. It's quite likely you already dislike me. Most young people do. Patrick, on the other hand, has always had a covey of young friends. It's no surprise to me that he has married you. You are pretty in a natural way. Everything for Patrick must be natural. Did you know he went through a phase where he wouldn't eat something unless he knew exactly where each ingredient came from? Oh my, Gracie, do you remember how thin he was then? Of course I cooked the same way I always did. I was stubborn. Still am, though age may have softened me some. I can't stand my own ground like I used to. Now I have to sit and let people do things for me. But I won't complain, will I, Gracie?"

Gracie shook her head and smoothed the cover on the armrest. She then smiled at me, which looked like a signal to speak.

I cleared my throat. "Well, I'm so glad to meet you. I hope both of you make yourselves at home."

Mother nodded once. "It's quite like Patrick to be out when we arrived. He was always hiding somewhere. How I used to wish we didn't have that cupboard under the stairs. Do you remember how he used to hide there, and then jump out suddenly, roaring like a lion? Oh, it made us scream. Where is he hiding now, Sandee? It's not that studio, is it? He saved the best room in the house for his doodle work. No doubt he lives there and leaves you out here. Gracie, could you please find me a cold glass of water? My throat is scratchy from all this dust."

"Oh, I can get that—"

Gracie patted my arm as she slid past me. "Never mind. You keep Mother company." She had a low, manly voice, and I realized it was the first time I had heard her speak since she arrived.

I sighed and turned to face the woman in the green armchair. She still had one hand on the rounded top of her cane. Her eyelids drooped so I couldn't tell if they were closed or squinted. I said, "Patrick should be home soon. He had to get something from his office at the college."

"Of course he did. He knew we were coming. There's no one who handles hellos and goodbyes worse than Patrick. Does he still sneak up on people?"

I grinned, thinking of Patrick's way of entering a room quietly and then joining a conversation as if he had not just arrived. "Well, yes, you could say that."

"Telling tales about me, Mother?" Patrick said from the doorway of the sitting room. I whirled around. Gracie stood behind him, smirking. She carried the glass of water to her mother.

The old lady put a hand on her chest. "You'd better revise your ways, young man. I'm getting too old for surprises. You'll soon put me in the grave."

Patrick walked over, gave his mother time to drink some water, and then leaned down to kiss her on the cheek. "If your heart fails, I'm certain you can talk it into life again."

She waved a hand. "Bah, that's your smooth talk." But she was blushing and looked her son over approvingly. "You're as tall as I remember, and that hair on your face doesn't quite suit you, but I suppose I can still show your picture around back home. Gracie, you did remember the camera, didn't you?"

She nodded. "It's in the car. I'll go get it."

As she left, Mother motioned to the roll of paper Patrick held. "Is that your excuse for not being here when we arrived?"

"This," Patrick said, unrolling the paper, "is a drawing I began shortly before Sandee and I were married." He displayed the drawing of the model, Kristen, her upturned face bathed in light as she sat on her knees, hands flat on the ground.

Mother squinted at it.

He turned to me, explaining. "I've decided to do a series. Kristen has agreed to model for me this summer."

He rolled up the drawing, and Gracie returned with the camera, so I did not have to respond, but I noticed Mother shooting me a piercing glance. I passed off my flustered behavior as a natural reaction to meeting the infamous in-laws, but later that night I wrote in my prayer journal something so honest that I hid it with my hand, even though Patrick was already asleep next to me. *Dear Lord*, I wrote, *I now know more about Patrick than I ever did, so why do I feel as if I don't know him at all?*

I became more at ease with Mother and Gracie as the week progressed. Mother enjoyed taking walks around the house, and I proudly pointed out each variety of plants in the flower bed. When I mentioned this to Patrick, he went to the store and bought four lawn chairs, which we set under the big oak tree. Being outdoors put Mother in a good humor, and we sat there whenever the weather permitted.

"Where's your artwork?" she asked one afternoon as Gracie and I brought out lemonade and cookies. Patrick had taken leave to work in his studio. "I haven't seen anything of yours yet."

"I draw at our figure drawing sessions, but other than that . . . there's nothing recent to show."

She pursed her lips. "Don't let my boy intimidate you. He's good at what he does, but he gets too absorbed in his work. Gracie used to do all the chores because he was always busy with his doodles. Isn't that right, Gracie?"

Gracie nodded. "He couldn't be talked away from his drawing desk."

"If he knows what's good for him, he'd spend more time with you and less time drawing girls in their bathing suits." She tapped her cane on the grass for emphasis.

I immediately came to his defense, "But he does spend time with me! Operas, museums, dinners out, quiet evenings looking at books. Did he tell you about our honeymoon? He rented a picture-perfect cabin on a lake." I crossed my legs and lifted my glass halfway to my mouth. "He's most romantic."

Mother bit into an oatmeal cookie. She swallowed and said, "All the same, it's not you on his drawings, Sandee."

I didn't give a response, and she didn't expect one, so when Mother nodded off half an hour later, I was surprised that Gracie took up the subject again.

I stood up to pull a weed from the base of the oak tree, and Gracie said, "I wouldn't let Mother get under your skin. She doesn't understand about artists and models and all that."

I looked at her, mostly to see what Gracie looked like when she was talking to someone other than Mother. She had arms crossed, chin up. Her eye sockets were not as deep as Patrick's, but I recognized the same darkness that covered any personal expressions. "Oh, Patrick is really very devoted to me. I'm not worried about that."

"Good." She paused. "I'm glad he's married. Mother didn't like him to be alone."

Oddly, at least I can see it as odd now, I came to his defense again, though my words weren't in my own defense. "Oh, I think he did all right when he was single. He's a good cook, and when he was my teacher, his clothes never looked mismatched or wrinkled."

Gracie nodded. "All the same, you keep him company when he would rather be alone. He needs someone like that."

I would have liked to continue this conversation, but I didn't know what to say, and Gracie picked up the book she brought along to read while Mother napped. I cleared away the lemonade glasses, and as I stood at the kitchen sink, filling it with soapy water, I got the idea that I had not been doing much to care for Patrick. Remembering the gifts, the expensive outings, time taken away from his own work, I felt very self-centered.

Patrick put his hands on my shoulders as I dried the last of the dishes, and I jumped in surprise. He gave me a kiss on the cheek and reached for a clean glass, intending to fill it with water. I twisted around in his arms, drew his head down with both hands and kissed him, my mouth pressing into him all of my new resolve to show my love.

When I was through, he laughed. "What's this? Did you miss me?" He jokingly looked at the clock. "One hour ten minutes . . ."

"Oh, be quiet." And I kissed him again, but this time the door opened and Mother's cane tapped the floor. I tried to back away, but Patrick kept an arm around me.

Mother tapped her cane again and moved forward. "Carry on, you two. It's only me needing to use the facilities." And she shuffled past us as quickly as I've ever seen her move. Patrick's eyes twinkled from inside those deep sockets, and he was about to follow Mother's suggestion when we heard her grumble, "Can't even walk around his house without getting in the way. It's a good thing I'll be leaving soon. An old woman needs a place to stay where she can walk as slow as she wants without coming across something not meant to be seen. I sure hope Gracie never gets married."

Patrick winked and smiled broadly, and I buried my face in his chest, trying to smother the laughter.

*

After Mother and Gracie returned to Arizona, I carried out my plans to show Patrick more love and devotion. I had actually written these plans out in a neat, numbered list in my journal, which I now used for personal entries as well as prayers. *1. Spend time learning about the Kristen series. 2. Try to appreciate it.* Loving and respecting his livelihood clearly followed loving and respecting Patrick. Being an obedient, submissive sort of person by nature, I found my own steps for a better marriage a relief as the former way I had—of just living side-by-side with my husband—came into sharper focus. I set about the task cheerfully, fixing a plate of banana bread and cheese for Patrick and then knocking on his studio door.

He invited me in, and I smiled, setting the plate where he could reach it.

"Thank you."

I glanced at the canvas in front of him. Patrick had just begun an underpainting based off the drawing of Kristen and a pile of sketches, some of which he had taped to the wall.

"Is this the first in the series?" I asked.

He did not stop painting. "Yes."

"And how many more will there be?"

He shrugged. "Don't know yet."

"Will Kristen be coming here to model?"

"Yes. Sometime."

"Oh." I let my eyes roam the room, but I was really imagining my list, and I decided to move right along to number three. *Prove that I like being in his company.*

"I've had an idea, Patrick," I announced.

He put down his paintbrush and looked at me expectantly. "What's your idea?"

"Let's have a little party."

His eyes narrowed. "Go on."

"Just a small party. Maya and Alan. Eric and Karina. Us. If the weather is nice, we can have it outside." As I talked, I began to wonder if my idea might have missed the mark. When I had written it down, with Patrick softly snoring beside me, I had thought that showing off our compatibility to friends would be the most obvious proof that I enjoyed his company. It seemed a sacrifice of sorts because I easily became anxious at social events, and he knew I would not throw a party on a whim. Now, with Patrick staring suspiciously at me, trying to discern an ulterior motive, I nearly stepped down. However, plans were plans, so I met his gaze with more determination than I felt.

"Are you sure?" he asked.

"We could buy a picnic table, and I could find some simple recipes. I could ask Maya to bring her famous potato salad, and—"

"Wait." Patrick stood up and held me at arm's length, squinting into my eyes. "Where's the Sandee I used to know? The one who speaks the truth with her whole face and doesn't like pretending?"

I wanted to open up, tell him about the list. I wanted to assure him that I was still the same Sandee he had married. *But*, part of me protested, *I am doing this to show my love for him.*

"Wouldn't a party be fun?"

He let go of me. "Sure. We'll have a party. I'll buy the picnic table tomorrow."

We stared at each other. I glanced at his painting again. "Could I get updates on your series? I'm really interested in it. You hardly ever talk about what you do in here."

I could almost hear him think, *You hardly ever care about what I do in here,* but he said, "Yes, of course, I'll keep you updated."

"Great!" I could think of nothing else to say, so I left. In the kitchen, I took out pen and paper and began to prepare for the party, thinking that I had failed at something, and now I could only continue forward, hoping to correct the bungled plan as I went.

The day of the party came replete with clear skies, temperatures in the seventies, and just enough wind to keep the mosquitoes and flies at bay. God must have known I needed encouragement. Maya and Alan arrived as I brought out a slow cooker loaded with pulled pork.

"Goodness, is this all for us?" Maya asked, giving me a hug. Alan set out the bowl of potato salad. "This is perfect timing," Maya continued, "I was just starting to feel blue about the summer being almost over. What a great way to cheer me up!"

Eric's pick-up roared to a stop along our curb, and he and Karina joined us, adding carrots and ranch dip to the feast. My guests talked effortlessly as I took care of the last items, and when Patrick finally made an entrance, smoothing down freshly-washed hair as he stepped out the door, greeting our friends with his sly and formal manner —"What a day for a picnic. What a sky! Deep enough to drown in"—I began to breathe more easily. In fact, the party progressed so well that I became a bit drunk on my own success. When Maya suggested we join some other faculty members for an informal gathering at a local bar and grill she and Alan frequented, I did not say no. Patrick looked at me strangely, but he took up the idea and convinced Eric that he and Karina could legitimately attend since he had received a teacher's assistant position in the art department for the upcoming semester.

"I'd rather go home," I whispered to Patrick as we followed Maya into the bar and grill.

He shrugged. "We're here now. It would seem strange to leave so soon." A hand on my back offered comfort, but not nearly enough to get me through the evening.

Faculty members I knew, and some I didn't, greeted us noisily. They scraped up a few chairs. I felt hot, sandwiched between Patrick and Ralph Michaels, an English professor who bore a convincing likeness to Mark Twain. I liked Ralph well enough, but I knew from experience that he pinned quiet, listening people into corners and subjected them to long, windy orations about many things. I cringed at the tone of delight he expressed in his greeting, "Sandee! Just the person I like sitting beside in a crowded restaurant."

Patrick had already struck up a conversation with an environmental science professor across our table. I turned to Ralph, bracing myself with a stiff smile.

"Say, have you met the new guy in the department?" Ralph asked. "He's sitting next to Robin. I've had some time to talk with him, and he shows a lot of promise. Striking sort of fellow. I hope he works out."

The young man he pointed to did indeed strike me as interesting. His appearance held nothing out of the ordinary, other than the fact that he dressed very neatly and apparently took great care to look good. He wore rectangular frameless glasses, and behind those lenses his brown eyes snapped with energy, studying everything in their path with such force and good will that I dropped my own gaze when he caught me looking at him.

As Ralph began a detailed account of the wretched condition of our nation's school system I looked at the new professor again. He was no longer looking at me, so I felt safe to study the eager expression on his face as he talked. So eager to please, but he showed zero uncertainty. Was I jealous? There I sat, hot and anxious, unable to pull myself from Ralph Michael's grip, exhausted from having planned and executed my own party. I hated the noise, the merry-making, the general air of unruliness. And there *he* sat, cool and bright, new but not detached, obviously enjoying himself. The curious attraction I felt toward him was not the fruit of jealousy. I had found my opposite.

I nearly told Patrick about my discovery as we drove home, but decided not to. The get-together had put him in a good mood, and he whistled a tune as he drove.

"You know, Sandee," he said, "I didn't think the party was a good idea from the first, but you pulled it off. I had a good time."

That evening I did not write in my journal, but I did mentally congratulate myself for making Patrick happy. I also foresaw the long road ahead, a road shaped by my efforts to please him. I yawned and put my head on the pillow. This road was nothing like the ones Patrick took on his thought-inspired drives. This road yielded exhaustion, and I could not expect to ever turn around and come back to those first months of effortless love.

The beginning of the school year offered many opportunities to "be public" with Patrick. I put up a good front of enthusiasm, and Patrick humored me. "Fine then, we'll fly off together into the bright company of our friends," he said. I wouldn't claim that I ever learned to enjoy myself in these social flights, but at most events I did find a niche fit for a person like me. Someone needed to listen. Many people can talk, but only a few people can really listen. One night I learned the distressing details of my former history professor's divorce. Another time an older female adjunct confided to me the mistakes she had made in training her two children. At first I was unaware of my reputation as a confidante; I considered the personal stories my price to pay for being shy and awkward. As time went on, I noticed the respectful nods people gave me on campus, the quiet looks that said "Hush" and "I'm grateful" in one glance. I began to attend meetings while Patrick stayed home to work on the Kristen-paintings.

I sat in the back row at a visiting writer's poetry reading. His words blew slowly about the room in a deep, melancholy manner. I closed my eyes briefly. Someone tapped my shoulder, and I stared wide-eyed into the kind, sharp eyes of the new English professor, Neil Anderson. He motioned to the empty seat beside me, and I patted it to assure him it was not taken. We had met before, obviously, but our conversations had never gone beyond the papers he asked me to copy or other such secretarial tasks. Now, conscious of his nearness, I lost the spirit of the poet, and could think only, stupidly, of my lack of self-possession as I twisted my wedding ring back and forth, wound my purse strap around my finger, tucked a strand of hair behind my ear twenty times.

When it ended, Neil said, "Whew, I didn't think he'd ever get through it."

I laughed, despite my nervousness. "What?"

"Those slow, prolonged vowels. He carried off each word like a pallbearer at a funeral."

I laughed again, searching out the poet with my eyes. "Shhh," I warned. "He's right there."

"Well then, I suggest we go over *there*." He pointed to a corner of the hall that served as a small library, complete with bookcases and easy chairs. I nodded and followed him because I did not have an excuse to do anything else.

He began the conversation by abruptly asking about Patrick's paintings. "Rumor has it your husband is working on something secret and brilliant. Will there be an unveiling in the near future?"

These rumors had not reached my ears, and I sat very still for a moment. "I don't know," I said finally. "He is working on a series. I don't believe it's a secret."

"Hmm," Neil studied me frankly, searching for insincerity. I held none, of course, and he must have known it. He leaned back in his easy chair, crossing his arms. "I've had the honor of talking to your husband a time or two. He doesn't say much, does he?"

I bristled, instinctively defending my husband's reputation. At the same time, I knew what Neil meant. Patrick did not, after all, say much, especially about himself and his artwork. "No, I suppose not. He's rather . . . choosy about his words."

Neil laughed, and his laughter had a contagious, merry sound which put me more at ease. "So are you, it would seem! He must have rubbed off on you."

"Oh!" I felt the heat rise to my face, but it was not unpleasant. "I've always been this way."

"A perfect match." He studied me from his laid-back position in the armchair.

I don't know what made me want to cry. Nor do I know what made me want to run for the door. I did neither. "Not perfect," I said.

Neil frowned. "Better than average?"

I shook my head. Shrugged. "I don't know. He seems so distant most of the time. I thought I knew him better when we first married. He has changed, or closed up, or," and by this time I knew I was treating Patrick wrongly, but I didn't care; I felt I was due these few complaints, "or stopped caring about me."

"That's sad, Sandee." Neil's expressive face softened in sympathy. "Are you sure he's not just . . . busy?"

"Yes, he *is* busy." Something in the way Neil said it reminded me of Patrick's mother. She had warned me about Patrick getting too absorbed in his work. That was true. Patrick had trouble pulling himself away from his paintings. And what did he concentrate on, hour after hour? Another girl.

"It's too bad," Neil said quietly. "Seems to me he's missing out on a lot."

I tried to laugh, but it came out choked. "Thank you." Wiping my eyes quickly, I picked up my purse and left.

I avoided Patrick most of the next day, not a difficult task. We rarely saw each other on campus, and after work I spent time in the flower bed, cleaning it out before winter. The brisk fall air kept me from melting into self-pity, but it did not keep anxious thoughts away. Our figure-drawing session would begin in a couple hours, and I did not know how I could act normally in the company of Patrick *and* Kristen. I considered staying home, pleading a bad headache, but I did not have a headache, and lying never seemed helpful in any situation. Instead, I arrived early and stopped at Maya's office.

"Maya," I said, tapping at her open door. She whirled around. "I have a question."

Maya put down her pen, her brow bunching at the sight of my sorrowful face. She beckoned me inside. "Did someone die?" she asked in a low voice.

I shook my head, almost smiling. "Not quite. I'm, um, having a difficult time with something. I want your advice."

She raised her eyebrows, ready to joke about something, but then she changed her mind and nodded. "Go ahead."

Sitting down, I sighed. "If someone really close to you started ignoring you because he was so busy doing something with another woman, would you do something about it?"

"Would I do something about it!" Maya threw both hands in the air. "The creep. Who is she?"

"Kristen."

"What?" Understanding dawned on Maya's face. She stared at me. "Let me get this straight. Kristen is not actually doing anything with him besides modeling, is she?"

I shook my head.

Maya tapped her long nails on her desktop. "And Patrick isn't actually talking about her to you, is he?"

"No."

"But you suspect there are stronger feelings involved?"

"I suspect nothing. I know he is with her more than he is with me. He's . . . obsessed with her."

Maya sighed. "Artists get that way sometimes."

"That doesn't help me. He's an artist, but he's also my husb—"

"I know it." Maya tightened her black sweater around her shoulders. She looked past me, into whatever plan she was formulating. "Try to make it through tonight. I'll keep my eyes on them. We'll talk about it later."

I stood to leave, and then I caught sight of a book at the top of a haphazard pile on the corner of Maya's desk. *Velázquez*. It was the same book Patrick had lent me when he came home from his sabbatical in France. I remembered how intensely those images had symbolized the feelings I felt for Patrick. I remembered *Las Meninas* and the man arrested in the doorway, looking at the viewer. At that time, I had associated Patrick with the man in the doorway. But now, in a flash of memories and insight, I imagined Patrick to be the artist himself, painting a portrait at his easel. The viewer could not see if the portrait was of the little princess or her royal parents, who were cloudily revealed in a mirror on the wall. In a leap of mental associations, I received the hope I most desperately wanted. Patrick might be painting Kristen, but what were his portraits really about? Were they really about Kristen, the friendly model with the thick braid and toothy smile? I knew Patrick's thoughts ran deeper. Everything in Patrick ran deep. The paintings, though I did not yet know their true subject, would bring to light the direction of his obsession.

"Maya," I said, staring at the book, "something just occurred to me." I shared, in faltering phrases, the awareness I had just received. She laughed, flipped to the painting in the book, and said, "Good ol' Diego. If only he knew the crisis he just deflected." She turned a more serious eye on me. "I'll still be watching tonight. You may be right about the paintings, but you have me worried. Patrick should know what he's missing."

"Thank you," I said, turning to leave. I walked quickly to the drawing studio, thinking about Patrick's paintings. Patrick may have been thinking about the same thing as he left the studio. We crashed into each other, my shoulder thumping against his chest. His arms steadied me. The woodsy cologne he liked to use in cool weather sent my senses reeling in sudden longing. I did not want to step out of his arms.

"Are you all right?" he asked, letting go of me. " I nailed you pretty hard."

"Yes, sorry. I don't know why I was walking so fast."

He studied me. "Hmm. You must have been thinking. About art."

His astuteness disturbed me. Was I that transparent? I raised my chin. "Yes, you're right again."

"Well." Patrick studied me again, and whatever he saw or felt as he looked right into my annoyance and worry did not register on his inscrutable face. He glanced at a clock on the wall. "We have time to talk. Come to my office."

Patrick's office served as an in-between station for his art finds before he uncovered a place for them at the house. With paintings and prints arranged tightly on all available wall space, posters and show bulletins pinned to the tack board, and small sculptures and reliefs lining the top of the bookcase, his office held the same crowded appeal of his sitting room. Our sitting room. I stared numbly at a print of one of Rothko's multiforms, the vibrant blocks of color breathing with me, like an abstract copy of my own heart. I knew Patrick, who had shut the door and then sat in the student chair next to me, was waiting for me to say something. I continued to breathe deeply, staring at the print.

"You know," he said at last, "I rather like this change of view. When I'm behind the desk, I don't see half the things my visitors can see."

"Maybe you ought to change your view more often," I said quietly.

He paused. "Sandee, I don't know what you mean. If you're upset about something, you should just tell me."

"I'm upset about something."

He groaned. "Must I pull it out of you? What is it?"

I answered with an intensely hurt look, daring him to see inside and find the pain he had caused. "What has happened to you? Why do you spend so much time . . . " I was about to say *with her*, but decided against it since I had changed my own opinion about that in Maya's office. I finished, "in your studio."

He drew in a sharp breath. Exhaled. "My paintings—"

"Yes, your paintings," I cut in. "Your wonderful, secret paintings."

"I've neglected you."

"Really?"

Our eyes met, and for the first time I was frightened by what I saw. Inside those deep sockets, his gray eyes flashed angrily. I could not tell what he would do.

He said, "Sarcasm doesn't suit you."

I looked away and stared stonily at the Rothko print, but its gentle, sensitive rhythms were lost on me.

"What can I do to appease you?" he asked. His tone had returned to its quiet rationality, but I could sense frustration in his lack of movement. "Shall we go out to dinner? Visit a museum? Plan a party?"

I was silent a moment. "Tell me what your paintings are about. Your Kristen paintings."

"Is *that* it?" He ran a hand across his face. "Why is that an issue?"

I still refused to look at him. "There are rumors circulating about your paintings. I think, as your wife, I ought to be in on the secret. Why do you keep things from me?"

He stood up suddenly, paced the small room, sat down at his desk, facing me. "I don't try, Sandee. Had you asked me, I would have told you all about them. There's no secret."

"Then, why not tell me now?" I challenged, but I felt the edge in my voice melt into sadness.

He shook his head. "Now is not the time. You aren't ready to listen." He studied me as I dropped my gaze to my lap. "Will you draw with us tonight?" he asked. "The others are probably ready by now."

"No, I can't," I said truthfully.

He understood. When I moved to leave, he got up to open the door for me. Squeezing my arm, he whispered, "We'll be okay."

I knew what he meant, and I was grateful. I left the building and walked to my car. As I sat in the driver's seat, I could not imagine going back to the empty house, so I sat, mentally replaying the argument. Soon Patrick came striding out of the building, head down. He did not see me; he was in such a hurry to leave. The tires squealed as he left the parking lot. I watched him go, then started my own car. I went to the house and waited for Patrick there, but he was gone a long time, and I fell asleep before he came back.

When I awoke, he was already in his studio. He left a note on the kitchen counter inviting me to join him there. Some of the injustice I had felt the day before came back to me. I did not want to come to him like a humble student before the great master, hanging on his every word, hoping to learn his secrets. I also didn't want to be angry anymore. I wrote on the bottom of his note, *Thank you, but perhaps another time. I hope you understand.* I didn't know how he could possibly understand, but it was the only thing I could think of to write.

Neil Anderson had his back to me when I stepped into my office. He was using the copy machine, and the noise deterred him from hearing me enter. I opened a drawer and slammed it shut. He looked up, startled. And then pleased.

"How are you, Sandee?" he asked.

I thought he deserved more than a flippant answer, so I paused, considering. "Fair," I finally said.

His eyes squinted in concern. "I hope things haven't taken a turn for the worse."

I shook my head. "No. Not really." I felt awkward saying more, but the way he continued to look at me made me add, "We've talked."

Neil knew instantly to whom I had talked. Laying down a stack of papers, he asked, "A good talk?"

Again, I shook my head. "It didn't amount to much."

"You look stressed out. Can I get you a cup of coffee?" He moved quickly to the coffeemaker on the side desk.

I laughed. "That's supposed to be my job!"

"We must take care of our excellent secretary," he said, measuring coffee into the machine. "What would we do without you?"

I laughed again. It felt good to be teased. Patrick's seriousness and obsessiveness surged mysteriously through my body. Those qualities had never bothered me before, but then, Patrick had also been attentive to me *before*. Before what? That was the question.

"Seriously now," Neil said, somehow sensing my mood, "you should try to relax. These problems have a way of working themselves out. In the meantime, don't work *yourself* out."

"Yes sir," I said. I had meant to say it in a cheeky voice, but it came out sincerely. I added, to cover my embarrassment, "Thank you for the coffee. That was kind of you."

Someone down the hall called his name. He turned to see who it was. Before he left the office, he quietly added, "You are a kind person. That is why I care about you."

I thought about his words for a long time. It occurred to me that some people might call his manner flirtatious. I did not find it so. Whereas people like Patrick might hide their generous feelings from people, Neil acted upon them. Neil did not strike me as person who could keep secrets. Conscious that I was comparing my husband to Neil, and confused by the implications, I threw myself into the never-ending pile of paperwork on my desk. I looked at the clock in surprise when Maya showed up at my office.

"Lunch?" she asked.

"We shortened the drawing session last night," Maya announced as we sat at a table with our salads and drinks.

"I suppose . . . just you and Eric."

She looked at me sharply. "Patrick walked in looking more upset than I've ever seen him."

I explained to Maya that we had a confrontation after I left her office. I did not go into details, nor did I encourage her to ask for them. The situation drained me, and I was ready to bury the whole thing, give my energy and nerves a chance to recharge, and then deal with it when it resurfaced. Maya did not look pleased. She stabbed her salad violently.

"Let's talk about something else," I suggested.

"Fine. Let's talk about Eric. He had an announcement to make last night, but then two of his friends weren't there to hear it."

I put down my fork and stared at Maya. "Maya, don't be mad at me."

"He and Karina are engaged," she continued. "He told me all about it. Eric is finally settling down."

I hardly knew what to say. I felt selfish.

Maya pulled out her cell phone. She found what she was looking for and passed it to me. She had taken a picture of Eric holding a drawing of Kristen. Even in the darkened snapshot, I could see the drawing had turned out triumphantly. The woman Eric had drawn stood straight, gazing into the far right of the page, a hand shielding her eyes. Sturdy, strong, and purposeful, from the heavy braid hanging arrow-like down her back to the carved sinews in her legs, this woman bespoke power and accomplishment. She bore all the heroic qualities Eric normally instilled into his figures, but she also bore grace. She looked as if she might fly to that far-away place in her vision.

"It's very good," I said.

"Go to the next picture," Maya instructed.

I did, and in the next picture I saw one of Maya's women, the same pose as Eric's but from a different angle. Maya had stationed herself very close to Kristen so that she was looking up at her face. Displaying the woman from the waist up, this portrayal drew its strength from the deep shadows beneath the shielding hand, the determined, unsmiling set of the lips, and the largeness of the hand itself. Maya's woman looked into the future. What she saw did not lighten her expression, but it did strengthen her resolve.

I handed the phone back to Maya. "You both drew well last night. I'm impressed."

She did not say anything for a minute. Then, as if she had mentally come to some conclusion, she said, "Eric's drawing is Karina. He's in love with her, and it shows. My drawing is you."

I blinked. "I'm not sure I follow."

"Silent, up against a lot of trouble, but not defeated, not giving up. That's you, Sandee."

I shook my head, irritated. "How can you even say that?"

Maya nearly hissed, "Because it's true. You're not the type to give up without a fight."

I let the words settle. When Patrick and I argued, it wasn't a battle with barbed words and double-edged swords. Instead, I felt the tug and pull of exhaustion and stubbornness, painful waves and undertow. Fighting and giving up did not appear as authentic possibilities. Keeping truth above water, not sinking into depression—that was the struggle. That struggle Maya would never understand.

"Thank you," I said.

"You're welcome."

We finished our lunch and returned to our offices. I checked my email and found a short note from Patrick: *Looked for you at lunch. Please be home tonight. I'll make dinner. We'll talk.* I would not have much time to rest before the next tide came in, trying to set me adrift.

✳

I arrived at the house agitated and with a headache. Dread devoured me as I opened the door, walked in, made eye contact with Patrick. He was busy at the counter, peeling potatoes. When I entered he looked up but did not speak until I hung my purse on the coat tree and rifled through the mail on the table.

"This reminds me of our first dinner together," he said. "I'm just as nervous."

I knew it had cost him some pride to admit his nervousness. I thought, *We are so alike, after all. Why did I think our love was falling apart?* And yet, I couldn't erase my own uneasiness. I gave him a small, tight smile. "May I help with something? Please."

He asked me to make pudding for dessert. I chose a box of instant butterscotch from the pantry and emptied its contents into a bowl, all the while trying to think of something nice to say, something to set us both at ease.

He put the pot of potatoes on the stove and adjusted the dial. He watched me stir milk into the mix. I poured the pudding into four bowls, and we both moved them to the refrigerator, Patrick holding the door open. When he closed it, I expected him to be looking at me, but instead, he was studying the art show poster for the collage-artist, the one I had left hanging for Patrick's sake when I first noticed the pretty rose wall behind it.

Patrick took it down. "You didn't like his art, if I remember correctly. Why did you leave it here?"

I shrugged. "Because *you* liked it."

He sighed and let the poster fall on the counter. "I think I've been a poor husband. And you are so good to me."

"That's not true," I said weakly, convincing no one, least of all myself.

He took a deep breath and attempted a smile. "Let's try to have a good time tonight. Like a dinner date. Like old times."

I felt the hopelessness of that suggestion, but I bravely nodded and reached to give his hand a squeeze. He led the conversation then, discussing a promising student, asking about my secretary work, commenting on the weather and the hustle and bustle at the grocery store that afternoon.

We did not talk about anything personal until we had finished our meal of pork chops, mashed potatoes and spiced applesauce. We took our bowls of pudding into the sitting room, and as I ate the first spoonful, Patrick said, offhand, "I'm on my last painting. Would you like to take a look?"

I nodded. "Of course."

In a terribly polite manner, he ushered me into the studio, our puddings left on the coffee table in the sitting room.

On his easel rested a painting of Kristen in a modest black dress. She sat primly in the exact center of a blue-gray couch, her hands folded in her lap, her bright face, erased of emotion but shining with freshness and youth, a flower in the heart of the painting.

He had lined his other paintings side-by-side against the wall. Six in all, I studied each one and for the first time saw beyond Kristen's face and personality. In each canvas, the woman bloomed, drawing attention not to herself, but to beauty within her, shining out. While I had thought badly of Patrick, he had created a world in which good presided. I felt deeply in the wrong, and tears came to my eyes.

Patrick's arms immediately came around me, and I let myself be held, enveloped in his open-air cologne, which took me back to our honeymoon in the woods and our long drives on lonely country roads. Patrick did not guess what I was feeling or thinking, but he murmured, "It's okay, we're okay," and he kept holding me close, tenderly stroking my hair with his hand.

Later, when he had fallen asleep, I wrote in my journal, *Dearest Lord, please give me your love, so I can love my husband. Grant me your wisdom, so I can understand his love for me.* I considered how close I had come to pushing Patrick away and replacing him with other things: my grudges, other people's intimate problems, and Neil. Glancing at Patrick, his body turned from me, a breathing boat in the wrinkled, wave-like sheets, I knew he carried secrets and wisdom that I would never comprehend. Earlier, his arms still around me, he had explained that the Kristen series arose from his desire to be young again. *You put that desire in me*, he said. I told him that I did not wish for or need him to be young. "I only wish you to be yourself," I said, "because anyone else would not suit me."

Patrick put a desire in me, as well—a desire to *seek out* truth instead of just defending what crumbs of it I already owned. I began by converting part of our kitchen into a small drawing studio. I drew by the clear light of the north window, pulling out old drawings and sketches and searching the busy, cluttered scenes for meaning and importance. Often I pushed my work away in frustration, went outside to shovel the sidewalks or sit at the picnic table, watching birds at the feeder. But then I came back.

When I sat down to draw something that was to become Eric and Karina's wedding present, I thought I'd try a picture of Eric at his drawing horse, measuring distances with his thumb. In the end, I wrapped up a small drawing of Kristen, taken from the sketch I had done the night Patrick asked me to marry him. Such a small, simple drawing—a young girl kneeling, her face turned up to the light—so unlike my other drawings. Those many things that came before. They were still there. Even when removed from the page, they shaped the truth of what remained. To Eric and Karina, I hoped the girl would represent a unity that surrendered to their inevitable differences, much as my unpretentious drawing formed a unity between the different versions of Kristen we had drawn.

As Patrick and I dressed for the wedding, I watched him out of the corner of my eye. Smoothing his goatee at the mirror, straightening the knot of his tie, he appeared normal, a little vain, a touch insecure. I caught his eye in the mirror. He stood still, expressionless.

"You have that look," I said.

"What look is that?"

"Handsome."

A smile grew on his face. He winked at my reflection.

I couldn't help laughing, but even as I came up behind to straighten his collar, I breathed a very serious and sincere sigh of relief. What love we shared had suffered blows, and yet, bent and wounded, it grew upward, fiercer than before.

Cezanne's *Sainte-Victoire Mountain*, circa 1897.

23966760R00105

Made in the USA
Charleston, SC
09 November 2013